Decisions Trilogy

Ralph M Edgerson Jr

ISBN **978-1-943159-25-3**

The publisher would appreciate notification where errors occur so that they may be corrected in subsequent printing and/or editions. Please send comments to the publisher by emailing to deeprivers67@yahoo.com

INTRO

It's been over three years since Ronnisha's funeral, and
her passing is still a sting to everyone associated with the
Daniels family but it's a driving force for Khori Daniels.
He has become a cannabis mogul in the marijuana industry,
being featured in several magazines, owning several acres
in Colorado where he is a prominent figure and also an
influential individual with young adults he inspires with his
foundation "Push Forward". A foundation he created for
young adults to become entrepreneurs, businessmen and
women, inventors and to hone their talents. Devin Daniels
has also made his mark at being considered the most
dominant Defensive End on the football field as he enters
his third year of professional football. He joins a new team
in Denver after winning his first Super Bowl in Houston
last year and is extremely excited to be the veteran player
joining a new group of young talented guys. But he also
uses his young cousin's passing as a motivational drive
with his "Nisha Foundation", where he helps talented and
at-risk teens reach their goals. Shalay Daniels and Kevin
Talport went from business partners to a loving power

couple as they moved forward with their relationship. The bond grew even stronger after Kevin introduced Shalay to his daughter Renee, who is 16 now. Shalay and Renee instantly connected, being that her mother abandoned her 13 years ago because Renee was diagnosed as being autistic and the only mother figure, she knew was her grandmother Maxine Talport. So, to have a much younger woman to interact with was a pleasure for Renee and a true healing process for Shalay. Alonna Daniels-Brooks and Steven Brooks celebrate their three-year anniversary on a cruise to Honduras, all the while getting ready to send their youngest child Dashanae to college next year. Cedric Daniels and Sherell Daniels are totally embracing married life with one another. Cedric vowed to himself that he would continue to show his wife how much he loves her every day, not relying on monetary means to speak for him like he did with his last marriage. Kareem Daniels and Yolanda Patton are completely enthralled in their precious three-year-old daughter Camille, who has become the light of their lives. Delores Daniels enjoyed seeing all of her children prosper in their lives, financially, emotionally and spiritually, it was all she ever wanted for them. But a nagging continuous occurrence of misplacing things, forgetting important moments or even confusing herself with a loved one's name brought Delores' children to the conclusion that they need to get their aging mother some professional help.

CHAPTER 1

The sound of the helicopter's spinning blades was deafening as Khori's Business Manager and lover Erica explained to him about one of his growing fields.

"Khori, the little guy sounded so nervous on the phone when he was explaining to me that he didn't want to bother you, but he had no choice", stated Erica as she handed him reports from his two other fields.

After flying over a large acreage of pine trees the helicopter came to a wide opening where a large greenhouse, two other buildings and a few trucks rest in the middle. As the helicopter made its descend to the ground, Khori's lead grower waited for them to land and approached the craft quickly opening the door.

"Hello Mr. Daniels, sorry you had to come out here, but I needed you to see this for yourself. I've tried everything and maybe you can figure out what's wrong with our hydroponic section", confessed an anxious young man by the name of Carl.

The trio of Khori, Erica and Carl made their way into the greenhouse where workers were rigorously working their stations as they seen the owner and CEO walk in. Carl showed Khori the problem he was encountering in the sectioned off Hydroponic Center of the greenhouse,

"Sir, we tried everything, but the plants have been browning. Sir, we checked for insects, water levels, nutrients levels and we haven't figured out the problem yet."

While inspecting his products Khori replied,

"You have an algae build-up either in your sprayer system or in the base mediums and it's suffocating the hydro. Clean out the system and add a grapefruit seed extract to the nutrients we spray our plants with. Second don't call me sir not one more time, my name's Khori bruh."

Khori smiled and headed over to the rest of the centers that made an arrangement of all types of marijuana, he even assisted in the clean-up Carl was in charge of. He seen all his employees were nervous with the boss being there and felt it was time for them all to relax. Khori called for an early lunch break, had his employees lunch cater to them and they all sat down to enjoy a meal together. After lunch Khori and Erica headed out after making sure everything was taken care of but an unexpected phone call to Erica shocked them both, as they boarded the helicopter.

Shalay was picking Zachariah up from his basketball practice, Friday afternoon, when her mother called,

"Hey mama, I was just about to call you. How's your day going?"

"I'm good baby real good. I know you busy but can you get mama some stuff from the store", replied Delores.

Shalay happily agreed to the task,

"Of course mama, what do you need? Me and Zach was heading to the store anyways."

Delores heard her daughter mention her grandson's name and immediately started talking about how proud she is of him and his siblings. After giving her grandkids praise Delores started to tell Shalay goodbye but Shalay remembered her mother needed her to do something for her.

"Mama, what did you need from the store. You asked me to get something, but you never told me", asked Shalay.

"I did baby? Don't worry about it, I'll get Alonna to get it", replied Delores.

Shalay really felt something was wrong because her next statement had her mother confused,

"Mama, Lonna on a cruise with Steven right now. Remember?"

Delores paused and was silent for a while but replied,

"She is? I guess she is. Well baby, mama just need some bread and that peanut butter I like."

Shalay agreed but really felt something was wrong because her mother has repeatedly loss her train of thought on several occasions in the past year or so, in her eyes. She called Cedric to confirm her assumptions and his answer scared Shalay because her brother told her of a few times their mother has forgotten his name or even called him someone else's name. Cedric informed Shalay that he has already scheduled a doctor's appointment, for Monday morning, just to have some test done and make sure everything is ok with their mother. The thought of her mother losing her memory or having a difficult time recalling her children's names affected Shalay in a drastic way and she didn't know how to handle it. Shalay has always, since a little girl, looked at her mother as being the strongest woman she knows and for her to have a weakness is hurtful.

Yolanda walked into the barber shop with Camille and the little three-year-old made a beeline straight to her father's office. When she walked in Kareem was on the phone with a client, but all business ceased when he seen his little baby girl's smile. As he was hanging up the phone Kareem picked up his daughter and sat her on his lap,

"What are you doing here little bit?"

"I was actually heading home to start dinner, but somebody kept yelling daddy in the car", replied Yolanda.

Kareem couldn't help but to kiss his little girl all over her face as he repeated,

"You wanted to see daddy? You wanted to see daddy?"

Camille's giggles were intoxicating as she was truly a happy toddler all the time. Yolanda knew Kareem had some things to take care of at the shop and told him that they would see him when he gets home but he insisted that he leave with them as he went over to his lead barber,

"J.B., can you close up for me? If not, it's cool."

J.B. had no problem closing the shop as he said yes and told everyone,

"Hey! I'm the boss today and I don't want no crap from y'all. Cause none of y'all want this smoke."

Everybody in the shop looked and burst out laughing because they all knew J.B. was a character. As Kareem was heading to the front door with his family, he told everyone,

"No matter how much he insists it was my idea, no parties after I leave."

Kareem knew it was falling on deaf ears because his crew always had friendly "get togethers" after hours just to unwind. His shop crew became his family outside his real family, and they looked at Kareem as the head of the household.

Cedric and Kevin were going over some last-minute spreadsheets they had to get done before the end of the workday when Sherell walked in the office,

"Y'all not done yet?"

"It's all his fault cause I been ready to call it quits", jokingly replied Kevin as he grabbed a stack of paperwork and headed out the door.

Cedric did the same as he walked up and kissed his wife,

"Almost done baby, just gotta get this to accounting."

The two dropped off their paperwork and headed to the garage with Sherell as Kevin told the married couple they were invited to dinner tonight,

"Shalay wants to do a fish-fry for Renee and Zachariah because they passed their final exams this semester. I'm a see y'all there right?"

"Of course, we'll be there", replied Sherell.

Kevin has truly enjoyed sharing his daughter with the Daniels family and they have accepted her with open arms. In the beginning Kevin was very protective of Renee because he knew she was a little different than most kids her age. But he also knew it was harmful for Renee to keep her away from society because he and his parents won't always be there to protect her. Educators and medical therapists diagnosed Renee with having Asperger syndrome, a low level on the autism spectrum, when she was just two years old. Kevin dove in educating himself on what his daughter was dealing with and the methods in which he needed to take in raising her. While Renee's own mother distanced herself from her own child and eventually leaving Renee with her grandparents one summer, never to return. Kevin was an only child, so to have another little one in the house was a joy for Martin and Maxine Talport who loved their little granddaughter dearly. Renee really enjoyed being around Shalay and her kids, especially Lenelle who was fascinated with the knowledge Renee had on animals. Lenelle would always ask Renee about any animal she could think of and Renee would happily tell her every detail about it, from where its origin originates all the way down to the animal's lifespan. The two were almost inseparable at times with their own conversations.

Devin was sitting in his new condo, looking over Downtown Denver, as his sports agent was on the phone with Erica discussing a potential meeting.

"Good afternoon Ms. Pleasant, my name is James Watson and I'm a sports agent for a few athletes here in Denver. One of my clients would really like to meet with you", stated Watson.

Erica was a little suspicious of the call because most athletes strayed away from the marijuana industry,

"Sport agent you say and who is your client?"

Devin could hear Erica's voice over the phone and took it from Watson,

"Hey Erica, I've been reading a lot about your company and I would love to meet up with you."

"And you are", asked Erica.

Devin smiled as he replied,

"Oh, James didn't tell you? I'm Denver's new football player Devin Daniels, I went to school with you and my cousin Khori Daniels, whose probably right next to you. So, I need this to be a surprise cause I miss my cousin and I miss you too, meet me at The Fairmont in a hour."

Erica tried to contain her excitement because she knew Khori hadn't seen any of his family, except for seeing Devin on TV during games, for a very long time. She informed Khori that he had a business meeting that just came up with a promising future client but Khori was a little reluctant,

"So how much does this one want me to invest? I'm not really feeling investing my money into companies that's not willing to invest in the foundation."

Erica knew Khori was very adamant about companies he interacts with contribute back to the community in some sort of way.

"No, this one wants to invest in you and Push Forward. Let's hear him out and afterwards make a decision on where we wanna go from there. The guy's name is James Watson, a sports agent for some athletes here in Denver", replied Erica.

As the two headed to The Fairmont hotel, Khori talked over some payment arrangements he wanted to set up for his three siblings,

"I don't want this to look like it came from me at all. We've been putting this money on the side for the past two years for them and I don't want it messed up."

Erica understood he was a little antsy about doing something special for his little brother and two sisters, but she's handled bigger deals than what he was asking,

"Dude, I got it. All three of their accounts have already been created, bank cards have already been mailed off by certified letter so that we know when they get them and each envelope has a letter from The Push Forward Foundation congratulating them on being selected as recipients of the scholarships, stop worrying."

Khori knew Erica would take care of everything he needed but just like his mother, he had to cross every "T" and dot every "I" when it came to his siblings. He hadn't seen them in over three years, and he felt it was finally time to reach out to them. Erica knew he was missing his family and felt this meeting would be exactly what Khori needed, a moment away from always just being business. Khori and Erica walked in The Fairmont hotel when the concierge greeted them at the door to escort them to the Atrium where James Watson was waiting for them. When the two walked in Watson made himself known,

"You made it, hello Ms. Pleasant. Hello Mr. Daniels, so nice to meet you. Me and my associate have heard a lot of good things about Kush Farms that we had to meet the man behind it all."

"And who is your associate", asked Khori.

"The best Defensive End to grace the football field in Louisiana, Texas and Colorado", replied Devin as he walked up behind Khori.

Khori turned around to see his cousin and the emotions flooded him like a runaway freight train as he grabbed him in a loving embrace.

Cedric was enjoying a home cooked meal at his sister's house with his family when Mrs. Evans called him with a disturbing message. Mrs. Evans told Cedric that her and another neighbor had to help his mother in her house a few minutes ago because she was wandering in the street in her gown talking to herself. Cedric and Shalay immediately headed over to their mother's home to check on her, while Steven brought Sherell and the boy's home. Shalay's heart was racing as they got close to their mother's home, imagining to see the worst. Cedric was convinced that something was wrong with their mother because her behavior was way off from the norm. Shalay asked her brother,

"Should we call Reem, so he can meet us there?"

"Not right now, I don't want to spook her with all of us there. Shay, I really believe mama is suffering from Dementia or something and if that's the problem we really need to get her some help", replied Cedric.

Shalay didn't want to believe her mother was having an issue like that but recent events have all pointed in that direction and she knew it. As Cedric parked the car, they could see all the lights were on in the house. When the two started to make their way to the front door Mrs. Evans came out of her house,

"Hey y'all, I didn't want to bother you, but I knew you would have wanted to know what was going on."

"Thank you, Mrs. Evans we really appreciate it", replied Shalay as she walked up to her mother's front door.

They walked in to find their mother sitting at her dining room table, wringing her hands and mumbling to herself. Cedric sat next to her at the table,

"Hey mama, we just passed over to check on you."

"Hey Kareem baby", replied Delores.

Shalay instantly started tearing up,

"That's Cedric mama. That's Cedric."

Delores turned and looked at Shalay,

"I know that girl, that's what I said."

Shalay was about to correct her mother but Cedric
interrupted her,

"So, mama, what you doing?"

"Oh, nothing baby, I wanted to cook something special for
Sunday's dinner tonight", replied Delores.

Cedric looked at his mother still wringing her hands,
calmly put his hands on top of hers and sympathetically
told her,

"But today is Friday mama."

Tears began falling from Shalay's eyes and down her
cheeks as she knew something was truly wrong with their
mother. The pain was evident on her face as Cedric
gestured for his sister to not show any worried emotions
and he continued comforting their elderly mother.

CHAPTER 2

After a stressful weekend of going back and forth to his mother's house to make sure she was ok, Cedric sat at the foot of his bed early Monday morning completely drained. Sherell could see her husband was not himself, spiritless to say the least and encouraged him to just take the day off. He refused to give in as he went to the closet to pull out some work clothes,

"Baby, I gotta go to work. Right now, it's the only thing keeping my mind off of the inevitable."

Cedric was referring to talking with his siblings about having their mother placed in a senior living home, so that they would have around the clock supervision of her. He had mentioned it to Shalay earlier and she was totally against the idea stating that it's a place for the forgotten. Shalay felt that a senior citizens home was for the elderly that no one wants, and she loved her mother too much to leave her there. Alonna had just got back from her honeymoon when she heard of the ordeal the rest of the family had been dealing with, but she agreed with Cedric's decision. Kareem was still on the fence about it because he didn't want the only memories his daughter has of her grandmother to be in an old folks home but he understood his mother needed help. Cedric made his way downstairs to the kitchen to find Lamaj feeding his little brother Tre some cereal for breakfast. The three males of the household all sat and had cereal while Sherell fiddled around getting herself ready for work. Lamaj still had a month to go before he started his 2nd year of college at Grambling State University. Sherell and Cedric couldn't be any more proud of the young man because of his academics along with the full football scholarship, he received. Tre on the other hand was the class clown, always having teacher calls at home and Cedric going old school with a belt to his backside, but little man was getting better. Cedric and his wife were heading to work right after dropping Tre off to school, but Delores' oldest son couldn't get her off of his mind. He made it to work after fighting through New Orleans' morning traffic to find police and paramedics assisting a disoriented elderly man sitting on the sidewalk in front of their building.

"Aww, that poor baby. I just hate to see that", stated Sherell as Cedric drove pass.

It really hit home with Cedric because a lot of what if that was his mother Delores ran through his mind and a meeting with his siblings was a must. He let the thought fade from him, for now, as he allowed his workload to fill up his day.

Devin was sitting in Khori's office, looking out the window at downtown Denver, just amazed at how far his cousin has come in such a short time. From the local weedman on campus, selling dimes to a business giant in the marijuana industry, selling weight. He knew Khori was good at what he did but he didn't know that his cousin was cooperate America good. Khori's Marijuana strands and

CBD oils were all over the states as one of the highest grades created by one company. Devin patiently waited while Khori was having a phone interview with a radio station about an upcoming event and summit meeting. The star football player couldn't be prouder of the man that was sitting in front of him as he watched how poised and confident Khori was as he worked. After the phone call was over, Erica walked in with a list of appointments Khori had to make for the day when he responded,

"Damn man, can I just chill today? I'm telling you; you make me do one more thing and I'm a quit. I'm fareal, I ain't gone give y'all a two-weeks-notice or nothing. I hate it here."

"Devin do you see what I gotta put up with? Get yo cousin", replied Erica.

The three sat in the office catching up on everything going on back home when Devin told them about his little brother Semaj opening up his own tattoo shop. Semaj was always into art like Khori's sister Ronnisha was, but he also loved the art of creating tattoos. Devin fronted him some start-up money for a shop in New Orleans and Semaj's shop "Artistic Creations INC" has been the spot to be for quality tatts ever since it opened. Denver's defensive superstar proudly showed them Semaj's IG page named "Spice101" which featured pictures and videos of all his tattoos. Khori had been wanting to get a design he had in mind of a moral for Ronnisha, but he didn't trust anyone to do it right,

"Looks like I'm a have to go holla at my lil cuz to get this work done."

Erica was happy her lover was considering going back home because he hadn't been back to the city since his sister's funeral four years ago and felt it would be good for him to see family again. She instantly got online to book a flight to New Orleans from Colorado airport after looking over his upcoming appointments. After a nostalgic walk down memory lane, Devin started to talk with Khori about the reason he originally came to him. He wanted their foundations to join together to create scholarships for needing kids in New Orleans and Denver. Devin had already started some small non-profits in New Orleans and Houston, but he wanted to go on a larger scale with his mogul of a cousin Khori. The Cannabis guru was the mind behind the product, but the business monster was actually Erica and Khori happily handed it over to her,

"Shid, if it ain't involving growing some weed with the kid, I can't call it, but I like it. Y'all work out the deal, I just sign on the dotted line where she tells me to."

"You be thinking I'm playing. This is what I gotta deal with all the time with him. Them suits don't know how to react when they talking to Khori cause he ignant", replied Erica.

Devin couldn't do anything but laugh as he enjoyed spending time with his cousin again.

Shalay was visiting her daughter's grave with a dozen roses when she seen a single white tiger lily resting on her tombstone, she knew Levi had come to visit. She still couldn't bring herself to talking with Levi since their daughter's death but was pleased that he still took out time to remember Ronnisha. Shalay sat there talking to her daughter as if she was sitting right there with her. She was telling her about her little brother and sisters but couldn't say one thing about Khori because they haven't had any words with one another since Ronnisha's funeral. Shalay tried to reach out to him via text, calls, emails and even letters but was faced with no response. She missed her eldest son very much, but it seemed like he had cut himself off from his family completely after he revealed that he felt it was his fault for Ronnisha's death. Shalay had wanted so desperately to have Khori back in her life but didn't really know how to reach out to him. She didn't follow the cannabis community and didn't know how mainstream Khori really was at the time. Shalay got herself together after saying goodbye to her daughter and made her way to her car when she got a call from Alonna about their mother. Shalay's twin told her that Delores' neighbor Mrs. Evans had to help their mother in her house after she found the elderly woman wondering up the street arguing with herself, again. The news bothered Shalay because she didn't want to admit that the family needed some real help with their mother.

"Sis, she's getting worse. Mama is almost 70 years old, and her mind isn't as good as it use to be. We gotta do something before she hurts herself", stated Alonna as she informed her sister that she's on her way to their mother's house.

Shalay agreed to meet her there after she check on some work orders from a nearby hotel she just acquired. She ended the call and texted Kevin just to get some encouraging words from him. No matter what the problem, Kevin always seemed to have the right things to say to make Shalay feel better about whatever she's going through. Shalay explained to him that she's going to be at her mother's house and won't be able to meet him for their lunch date. Kevin replied,

"Baby go take care of ya mama. I got a lot of work to take care of anyways. Just keep me up to date, love that old lady."

Shalay just smiled at the text and let her brothers know, through a group text, that they all need to have a talk about their mother. Cedric already started to put everything in motion with a specialist to have test done but Shalay was still unsure about putting their mother in a home. After hearing story after story of neglect and abuse going on at old folk's homes, Shalay was very hesitant to send her mother to one. She had a temper when it came to the safety of her family and she knew if anyone was to hurt Delores that things would turn violent real quick. She had confidence that her brother knew what was right for their mother and that he did his research on the home he picked out. Shalay just had to get her head around the fact that her mother may be in need of around the clock assistance.

Kareem had just walked in the shop when he received a text from his sister about a meeting they had to have about their mother. Just like his sister Shalay, Kareem was a little indecisive about placing his mother in an elderly living facility. But he also knew that none of them were capable enough to handle the day-to-day activities of looking after their mother if she gets worse. Kareem didn't know about the recent incident that took place earlier that morning and called his mother just to check on her. The phone rung a few times before Delores answered and Kareem jokingly asked her,

"Hey old lady, you staying outta trouble over there?"

"Hey my baby. I would be doing just fine if my nosey neighbor stay her behind in her house. She's always over here, just a rambling her mouth. I just wanna watch my stories", replied Delores.

Kareem laughed as he continued to talk with his mother, and she went on about her neighbor's little dog constantly barking in the morning at the kids going to school. To him she seemed completely fine, holding a normal conversation like she has always done but just like the conversation was going smooth it started to veer off. Delores went down memory lane as if it was something that happened recently. She began an incoherent mixture of stories of past times when Kareem and his siblings were young, but it didn't make any sense to him because they weren't talking about any of that in the original conversation. It was as if Delores' mind was going through a rolodex of memories all at once, talking about whatever came up and Kareem had had enough of the rollercoaster ride as he told his mother he had to get back to work. It worried him something serious as he tried to figure out why his mother was going through what she was going through, if it was stress or just old age. Kareem started to think about if it was hereditary, if when he gets up in age would he be a worry for his daughter Camille, and it all came crashing in on him. He started searching online about Alzheimer and dementia, to get a better understanding of the symptoms and a better understanding of what his mother is going through. Kareem sat in his office for what felt like the whole day reading doctor's articles and studies of the disease, looking for one glimmer of hope in the situation. It was a good thing he had competent employees that could run the shop without his assistance because the only time Kareem looked up from his computer was when he received a call that a package was coming for him. When Kareem looked at the time, he realized that the majority of the day had went by and that he hadn't done not one assignment in the shop, but he had a better understanding of what Alzheimer was. He walked up front to see what his barbers and beauticians were doing when one of his stylists, who could see the strain on his face ask,

"Reem, you good? You been in the back all day. You really trusting J.B. not to burn the shop down. You know that boy special, he need supervision."

"J.B. been with me since day one, if he don't know nothing he know how to do this but you know you my back-up plan baby girl", smiled Kareem.

The shop was running smooth as Kareem looked over a few receipts and this sexy chocolate young lady walked in with a fairly large box in her hand asking for Kareem. When he saw her, he knew it was the package he had been waiting on to be delivered. Kareem was a barber by craft and a businessman by choice, but he wanted to venture out pass what he already has, to create something new for his brand. He had been studying different straight razor kits and the pretty delivery woman just sat his next study project on his desk. Kareem had one of his good friends of a friend find him some premium razors on a "five finger" deal that he wanted to look over when he began some small talk with the delivery girl. She was ridiculously attractive, and he noticed she had some well managed dreadlocks like his, so he offered her to come back to get a free style one day. It wasn't that Kareem was trying to flirt at all, but it was a good change of scenery to have something else on his mind other than his mother's issues at the time. Besides, when he found out the pretty face was the same age as his nephew Semaj, Kareem started to think of becoming a matchmaker, anything to avoid the present state of mind.

After his morning meeting with his team and a good workout, Devin was relaxing in his condo getting a deep tissue massage from a professional masseuse. He was enjoying the rub-down when he got a call from his mother and his muscles went from completely relaxed to tense all over again. Alonna didn't want him to hear it from anyone else but she didn't want to upset her son as she told him about the issues his grandmother had been having. Devin immediately began getting things together to head back to New Orleans while on the phone with his mother,

"Mama, I will be there as soon as I can. I'll let coach know I gotta go for a few days."

"Baby don't stress yourself out and come all the way here. You have a game coming up Thursday and another one right after that Sunday night. I need your head in the game, right along with my 3 sacks a game and maybe a forced fumble. I just wanted you to know and it not be a surprise when you get here next month", replied Alonna.

The stress was already there as Devin thought about his family going through yet another trying time. He tried his best to stay strong for his mother, letting her know he will complete everything she wants him to do during the football game, but the worry had already set in. Devin knew this was the opportune time for Khori to make an appearance back in New Orleans and mend any hardship feelings. He understood his cousin's reasons for separating himself away from his family, it was a healing process everyone had to go through, especially Khori. But Devin knew that everybody needed to be together for Mama Dee. Devin called Erica because he knew her cute dimples would always get Khori to do exactly what is needed to be done.

"I'm on it Dev. We were already talking about heading out that way next month for your game but I'm a get him there in a few days", stated Erica.

Devin was confident that Erica knew how important this was for him, that his cousin get back home as soon as possible. He went back to trying to relax before he had to head out to practice but the ringing thought of his grandmother not being herself picked at him. Devin so wanted to just fly out to New Orleans just so he could lay eyes on his grandmother's face, but he knew he had responsibilities in Denver. Delores meant so much to everyone in her family that her present state was affecting them all in some form or fashion. Her oldest grandson especially because he could remember when he was very little waking up for school and smelling his grandmother cooking breakfast for everybody in the house. Delores would be the first face he sees when he would come home from school and the last face after saying his prayers for bed. Not taking away from his own mother Alonna because she did everything she possibly could as a teen mom, but Delores was the grandeur of what a grandma was. Her love for her kids was felt in every way, from the praise for great accomplishments to the discipline for failures. Delores did everything in her power to give her kids right along with her grandchildren the means to be whatever they wanted to be, and she backed them all the way. Devin's grandmother was there for every main event in his life and to think that she is going through a truly trying time, he really just wanted to be there for her like she was for him all his life.

CHAPTER 3

It was a normal Tuesday morning and Cedric was at work doing his usual when he got a frantic call from Alonna about their mother. Cedric immediately started looking for his keys when Alonna told him that a fire broke out in the kitchen of Delores' house. The elderly mother was cooking breakfast, like she always did, when she got distracted by children laughing outside, walking to school. Because she was concerned that the kids would get chased by her neighbor's little dog, she watched them stroll up the street. After observing all the adorable little kids pass by her house, Delores sat in her living room to look at the early morning news. The big mistake was that she forgot she had bacon sizzling in a skillet on her stove. The bacon had burned to a black crisp and the grease had gotten so hot that it ignited into flames. Delores didn't notice the fire until a smoke detector sounded off but by that time it was too late, her stove and the wall behind it was engulfed in flames. She tried to put the fire out by throwing water at it, but the flames grew larger as the heat from the fire blew in her face. Smoke could be seen bellowing from the kitchen window as the flames increased and the ever so concerned Mrs. Evans could smell smoke in her own home. When Mrs. Evans went to investigate, she noticed the up in age Delores standing in her backyard trying to pull her water hose towards the smoke filled back door. Mrs. Evans shouted for Delores to stay away from the back door as she reached for her phone to call the fire department, but the little old lady went in the house anyways. While still on the phone with the 911 operator, the scared neighbor darted after Delores to pull her out of the burning home. The distraught elderly mother tried her best to put out the fire, scorching her hand in the process, as Mrs. Evans pulled her to safety and the sounds of a fire engine could be heard roaring up the street. Ahead of the fire truck was an ambulance halting to a complete stop across the street from the fiery house. The sounds of wood cracking under the pressure of the flames could be heard from the street as grey smoke reached to the morning sky. New Orleans Firefighters scurried by in their light brown uniforms, getting all the tools they needed to conquer the blaze in the back of the house. Delores sat in the back of the ambulance watching the firemen fight off the now large blaze that took over the backside of her home. The paramedic was tending to her wounds when a terrified Alonna ran pass looking for her mother and was turned around by NOPD officers. The crying daughter imagined the worst when she quickly walked up to the medical truck to find her mother in good spirits making the medical assistant laugh at her jokes about having a barbecue. Alonna stood there completely relieved to see that the only thing that was damaged was her mother's ego. The firefighters achieved the mission of putting out the fire as a fire marshal approached Alonna who was waiting with her mother. The gentleman informed Alonna that the inferno started at the stove and then advanced to the walls. Delores was telling her daughter that she was fixing herself some breakfast when Cedric finally made it to them. Listening to his mother explain the incident to them pushed Cedric to the decision that she needs around the clock help and Alonna was right in agreement with him. After the firemen finished their job and the back part of the home was sectioned off from the outside, Delores' kids prepared to bring her to their home.

Alonna wanted her mother to come by her because Alonna's husband Steven worked from home a lot and that would mean someone would always be there with her. Cedric was in agreement with her and none of their other siblings were against it after they heard the news.

Kevin was at a parent teacher meeting with his always joyous daughter Renee, as they talked with school officials about the progress Renee is having at school. He was always proud of any accomplishments Renee achieved in class and couldn't be any more proud when her teacher had nothing but good things to say about her. But the joy of the meeting all fell to animosity when the assistant principal told Kevin about Amanda LeBlanc contacting her about Renee. Amanda is Renee's biological mother that abandoned her 14 years ago and Kevin was livid that she had the gull to contact his daughter's school. The principal couldn't do anything but sit there silent as Kevin ranted,

"Ma'am I understand that you have many jobs to do and one of your jobs and your administration's job is to make sure my daughter is safe and secure in your facility. Ms. LeBlanc is in fact her birth mother but hasn't been a factor in Renee's life for over a decade and I would like to keep it that way. I shouldn't have to say this, but I will, please don't talk about my child to that woman again. If I find out that my daughter's safety has been compromised in anyway because of the negligence of this school, my lawyer will be contacting you. Am I completely clear on this matter?"

The principal continuously apologized for her actions and even told Kevin that she didn't give Amanda any information on Renee, even though she asked. Kevin ended the meeting as he escorted his loving daughter out of school for the day, but he was still agitated that Amanda tried to contact someone about his child. Amanda LeBlanc was a very well-off woman, not because of anything she did herself but because of her wealthy family that owned companies all over Louisiana and Mississippi. Even in high school where Kevin first met Amanda, she held up an image that she was Southern royalty and made it known she didn't bother with commoners. The LeBlancs and the Talports pushed for the teens to be a couple, because two prominent families joined together by marriage makes for a great combination. But Amanda didn't really care for Kevin's taste in friends because he enjoyed being around colleagues that Amanda felt were beneath him in status, even though she really liked him. Behind closed doors Amanda was everything Kevin wanted, sweet, sexy, smart and ambitious but her attitude towards the everyday person or less fortunate was less to be desired. In her junior year of college Amanda gave birth to their little baby girl Renee and the couple started talks of marriage. When Renee was just one, Kevin noticed his daughter was a little different than the other kids, but Amanda was completely blind to the fact or just ignored it. After a few visits with her grandparents, Martin and Maxine Talport, Renee was scheduled for an exam by a family doctor that specialized in child development because Kevin's parents seen the same thing. When Amanda got word that her only child may have a disability, the young mother blamed Kevin for not taking care of his body, exposing himself to unclean people and getting her pregnant with "insufficient sperm". Kevin couldn't believe the person he was in love with was that self-centered and uneducated that she would blame a disability like autism on something so ridiculous. Two months had passed since Kevin and Amanda got the news that their daughter Renee was diagnosed with functioning or high-functioning autism. The young father dove in educating himself with the spectrum, talking to doctors and specialist on the matter, trying to get a better understanding, while Amanda slowly distanced herself away from it. She couldn't understand why her daughter out of all the kids in the hospital had to be what she considered the sick one. Amanda loved her daughter but at the same time knew she was not ready to raise a child that would have challenges and her upholding a specific image became an issue. Being a trendsetter, fast pace entrepreneur, businesswoman and all didn't have a handicapped kid involved in Amanda's picture. One morning she brought 2-year-old Renee, with her favorite stuffed bear and a carry-on bag to her grandma Maxine, stating she'll be back in a few hours. That was the last time the Talports seen Amanda LeBlanc. The resentment Kevin had for Amanda could only be compared to a lion and a hyena, he couldn't stand the thought of her trying to come back into Renee's life.

Yolanda was in her office going over some details for a school field trip when her sister Denise called, telling her about her new house. After leaving Jamal, Denise stayed with Kareem and her sister until Yolanda gave birth to her daughter Camille. Denise stayed close around just in case her only sister and Kareem needed any help with their newborn baby. Even though she wasn't living in the same house as Jamal, she still had to see him every day at work but Ashley's father knew Denise had nothing to tell him. Jamal tried everything to get Denise back with him, but every advance was met with stern rejections, Denise couldn't see herself with a man like Jamal after the Ronnisha incident took place. She made sure to keep her distance from him right along with keeping her daughter away from him also. Once Jamal had realized he would never be with Denise again, he began to request to see his daughter. Denise did everything she could to avoid Ashley from being around her father, but the courts awarded Jamal joint custody. Denise did the one thing that she knew Jamal wouldn't be able to do and that was move to another state because Jamal had too many ties in New Orleans. She got a higher paying job at NASA Space Center in Houston which was just a lateral move for her from the NASA Assembly Facility in New Orleans. Denise didn't want to leave the only family she had left in New Orleans, but she needed a new start and better opportunity for her daughter. She knew Jamal couldn't follow her to Houston and his influence on Ashley would be limited to holiday or birthday visits. Yolanda listened as her sister painted a beautiful picture of the new home she just signed for,

"The house is huge! Four bedrooms, so when you and the fam come to visit y'all will always have a place to stay. I can't wait to send you the pics after all the furniture is in."

"Four bedrooms? Girl, it's just you and Ashley. You gone lose my baby in that big ass house", responded Yolanda.

The two sisters just enjoyed each other on the phone as Denise told her proud big sister about the neighborhood, the school and even her great new position at her job. Yolanda didn't want to, but she felt she had to mention to Denise about the challenge the Daniels family is facing right now with Delores. The news hit hard when Denise heard about the fire and she immediately asked how her ex-husband Cedric was handling it all,

"Ced puts on a good front that he's okay but keep an eye on him for me sis. He will stress himself out behind his family."

Denise knew her and Cedric could never be together again, but she still held strong feelings for him. They stayed friends even after the divorce was finalized and Sherell even had Ashley over for play dates with Tre. Denise and Sherell became closer once Kareem's baby mama revealed her pregnancy to the family. It all would seem strange to someone on the outside looking in, but forgiveness and acceptance ran deep in the Daniels family. Yolanda had a few parent meetings to attend and told her little sister they would talk later as she got off the phone. Denise didn't want to step out of place, but she had to hear her ex-husband's voice to know that he's not straining himself out. She knew how much Cedric cared for his mother and how much she meant to him, plus Mrs. Delores meant so much to her as well. Denise called Cedric's cell but was met with the answering service and she didn't know if she would find the same calling the twins. The concerned Denise reached out to Sherell to find her still at work going through serious anxiety because just like Denise, she couldn't reach anyone at the moment. The two women consoled each other as ideas of what may have happened at Delores' house ramble in their minds. Denise tried to alleviate some of the pressure of the unknown with questions about Sherell's little active boy Tre.

"That little clown is gonna give me every grey hair I get from here on. Girl, that little bugger never stops, do you want him? He comes potty trained and his own clothes, I'll even thrown in his favorite cereal", responded Sherell.

The ladies laughed as Denise told Sherell about her crazy active 6-year-old Princess Ashley and her assorted tutus. The conversation did its job as it relieved a lot of the worrying the women were going through and Sherell ended the call telling Denise she will keep her informed on all that's going on.

Semaj was at his tattoo studio getting things together before his other tattoo artist arrived when he heard about the kitchen fire at his grandmother's house from his stepfather Steven. He was about to drop everything and head to his grandmother's aid, but Steven told him that Alonna and her siblings had it all under control. Steven figured too many people there would be too confusing anyways and informed Semaj that he would keep him up to date on everything. Worried all the same, Semaj stayed put but called his brother Devin to let him know of the events going on. Devin knew about the incoherent conversations and wondering incidents but was completely bothered when he heard of the fire. Semaj could hear the strain in his brother's voice as he stated,

"Say bruh, I'm a have to get back home sooner than next month. Mama wanted me to wait til I'm down there to see granma but shit getting outta hand. I gotta make sure to tell Khori."

"You talked to Khori? When? He in Denver with you", asked a surprised Semaj.

Devin told his little brother that he wanted it to be a surprise to the whole family that he brings him back home, but he sees that Khori may need to make an appearance before that. He told Semaj that he got in touch with Khori as soon as he moved to Denver after his trade to his new team. Devin's little brother was shocked to hear how popular his cousin was in Colorado and surrounding states. Semaj looked up the botanical genius, on the Internet, known as Khori "Kush" Daniels to find several articles on the entrepreneur's adventures in the cannabis industry. He was completely caught off guard that his cousin was hiding in plain sight from his family. Semaj heard partial parts of the story behind Ronnisha's passing and how she was an innocent victim of some street beef. He didn't hold any grudge against his cousin for the act because he knew Khori wouldn't want any type of harm to come to anyone in his family, especially Ronnisha, in the first place. Semaj told his brother to give Khori his number because he really wanted to connect back with his big cousin and that he would keep their secret on the hush for now. Devin ended the call with his little brother and told him he will see them all real soon. Semaj prepared his shop to open up in a few as he let in his co-workers and went to his back office to get his mind straight. Thinking about his cousin Khori coming back home was a joyous idea but it was clouded with worry over how his grandmother was doing. No one was exempt from concerning themselves about the welfare of the Queen of the Daniels family. Semaj started to do the same as his uncle Kareem and educate himself on all the things affecting his grandmother. It all scared him to think that his grandma was losing her memory, the one thing that Semaj enjoyed so much as a kid was the stories of yesteryear she would tell. Customers started to pour in the studio and Semaj went straight into artistic mode as he listened to one of his clients describe a tattoo they wanted. His family's issues rested in the corner of his mind like a dark shadow as he sketched out intricate designs in a nearby sketchbook.

CHAPTER 4

Delores' children were all waiting in the conference room for Dr. Jackson to arrive. Shalay nervously twiddled her fingers as she sat between Alonna and Kareem, who were trying their best at keeping her calm. Cedric was just as nervous as his older sisters, but he didn't want to show it because he had to be strong for the rest of the family. They all didn't know what to expect the doctor to say but they all knew after the kitchen incident that they needed help with their mother. The small fire scared Shalay straight and she had no quarrels about having her mother placed in a senior living facility. The only thing they all wanted to know now was where do they go from here and what treatments were available. A middle-aged gentleman walked in dressed in a dark blue suit accompanied with mahogany leather shoes and matching ebony colored cuff links. He greeted everyone in the room as he spoke,

"How y'all doing? I'm Dr. Jermaine Jackson and before you ask, no I'm not related to the famous family. But for some reason my mama liked the name Jermaine."

The spill was a little funny because Dr. Jackson was a white man that looked nothing like the famous Jackson family. The joke eased everyone's tensions a bit as the doctor began to discuss what was going on with their mother. Cedric was introduced to Dr. Jackson by Kevin who did some extensive research on doctors who specialized in the study of dementia and Alzheimer patients. Dr. Jackson was the top specialist in the field in the city of New Orleans and the doctor held back no punches as he explained the disease to them. He explained to them the mortality rate of the disease first giving the worst-case scenarios, then calmed them with treatments and options they could take. The doctor let them know that it won't be an easy journey and that even though they may not feel like it now but some of them may even want to give up. Shalay thought to herself, she could never give up on her mother and took offense to Dr. Jackson's statement as she replied,

"Sir, I don't know who you are used to dealing with, but we won't give up on our mother."

"That's the spirit I need to hear but I'm a need that same energy all the time even when she gets violent", stated Dr. Jackson.

The facial expressions on the Daniels let Dr. Jackson know they weren't ready for that when he explained to them what he meant. He told them that they have to put themselves in that person's place and realize that their mind is not operating on a normal level. That a lot of times the person is filled with confusion and most of the time confusion is addressed with aggression. Cedric and his siblings all hoped they were up to the task at hand, but Dr. Jackson definitely gave them the impression he was more than ready. As everybody contemplated their roles to the upcoming, Kareem walked up to the doctor, gave him a firm handshake and thanked him for helping them with their mother. The doctor took them on a tour of his facility, as he showed them different treatments and medical practices they perform on their patients. Shalay looked at the place like a big science lab that was just there to practice experiments on her mother but when Dr. Jackson brought them to the actual living area of the facility Shalay was relieved. She seen other elderly men and women relaxing in makeshift single dwellings like it was their own personal apartments, with everything they would desire. Alonna asked about the living quarters, in reference to a kitchen area because of the thought of her mother having another accident. Dr. Jackson informed them that he has cooks on the grounds of the facility for all meals and everything is cooked by professionals.

"The transition may be a little difficult for Delores in the beginning and I encourage you all to be here because familiar faces will lessen the burden for her. I've ran across some that are completely comfortable here the first day and I've had some that fight me tooth and nail every day. But with your smiling faces and warm hearts she's gonna be just fine, I promise", stated Dr. Jackson as he held the hands of tearful eyed Shalay.

Delores' sons and daughters all headed home for the day before it started to rain because the sky was full of angry rumbling dark gray clouds. But nothing could rain on how good they felt about moving their mother to the senior living facility they just visited.

After hearing the disturbing news from his cousin about his grandmother, Khori caught a flight to New Orleans the following day. He was nervous as hell walking through Armstrong International Airport, not because he hadn't been home in four years but because he hadn't spoken to his mother in those four years. Khori and Erica waited at the pick-up area for their driver to arrive when Khori argued,

"Okay, this is stupid. Why do I need a driver? I know my city like the back of my hand. I can drive my damn self."

"Bruh, you need a damn driver because your gross income last year, on weed alone, was 1.8 million dollars and your CBD oils were almost twice as much. This guy isn't just a driver, he's an armed bodyguard that uses driving as a side hustle", jokingly replied Erica.

Khori didn't want to believe he needed security in his own hometown, but he understood where Erica was coming from. The Crescent City's night sky gave way to a serious thunderstorm as the driver made his way down Interstate 10 through New Orleans. Khori looked between the raindrop filled back passenger window at the city he called home for so long and felt like a tourist. Erica was too busy answering emails on her laptop to realize her partner was reacting to being back home in a somber way. The ride to The Ritz-Carlton Hotel was quick and the couple got themselves settled in when Khori stood at the balcony window, looking over the city. Erica walked up behind him and made the statement,

"Last time we were in a hotel here you took me on a tour of the city. I'm a need that same treatment sir."

Khori started smiling thinking about the fun they did have on Erica's first visit to the city with him. The memories of them touring the streets of New Orleans were pleasant until he thought about the reason they originally came to the city. Khori hadn't thought about the church incident afterwards or the whereabouts of Garu in a very long time. He tried finding the guy that was responsible for his sister's death, but it was as if Garu disappeared. The thought of Garu getting away without any consequences was heartbreaking and also the fuel that drove Khori to always remember his little sister in everything he does. He made sure Ronnisha's presence was felt with everything he created. All the way down to one of his most popular oils having her namesake "Nisha's Oil", which held the U.S. Hemp Authority Awards Seal and Khori prided himself in always keeping her close to his heart. Now being back home, he knew he had to rebuild the bond he and his mother had so long ago. With a grin Khori reminded Erica of their first time in New Orleans,

"We did enjoy touring the city but what I remember most is the showers."

Erica smiled, showing off those adorable dimples, as she began to unbutton her blouse, right along with her skirt and told Khori to meet her in the shower. Once he heard her start the shower Khori made his way to the bathroom to recreate their first time in the city but this time he won't be leaving in the middle of the night.

        Kevin was chilling at home with his daughter, looking at TV during the downpour, when there was a knock at his door. He wasn't expecting any visitors when he asked who was there and a familiar voice on the other side of the door brought an instant chill to his body. When Kevin opened the door there stood Amanda LeBlanc staring him eye to eye. It was as if the storm clouds announced her ominous presence with a thunderous crash and lightning strike. With the rain still crashing at her back Amanda asked,

"Are you gonna invite me in or do I have to just stand here in the rain?"

Kevin stepped to the side as he allowed her to come in, Renee greeted Amanda with a smile and a hello, not knowing who the strange woman was her father had just let in. Renee's estranged mother stood there amazed at the beautiful teen that sat in front of her. Amanda almost teared up a little thinking about the years she missed out on with her daughter as she just smiled back at Renee. She wanted so much to just run up to Renee and wrap her arms around her, but Amanda refrained from the thought. Kevin had enough of the emotional moment as he blurted out,

"Amanda, why are you here? How the hell did you get my address?"

"Well hello to you too Kevin. I came to talk to you about something very important to the both of us", replied Amanda.

Kevin asked Renee to go to her room so that he and the mysterious woman could have a serious conversation. Kevin sat down, at his dining table, as he watched his precious daughter walk down the long hallway to her bedroom. Amanda took off her raincoat and hung it on the coat rack near the door before taking a seat at the same dining table as Kevin. As always, Amanda was dressed in the finest garments all the way down to the red bottom heels on her feet adorned with a luxurious diamond necklace and matching tennis bracelet on her wrist. The parents of Renee sat across from each other like opposing teams on a football field as Amanda began to tell Kevin the reason for her visit. He listened as Amanda spilled out that she regrets not being in Renee's life and that leaving her was the biggest mistake she could have ever made. Kevin didn't interrupt Amanda not one time as she outlined the past 14 years and what lead her back to New Orleans. See after Amanda left Louisiana, she found herself in Las Vegas as a consultant, where she met her fiancé Alex Rideau and she felt she needed to reconnect with her whole family. Renee wasn't the only one Amanda left behind when she left but unlike her own daughter she did keep in contact with her parents, just to let them know she was alright. Kevin was thrown for a loop as Amanda told him that she wanted to become a part of Renee's life now and wanted to introduce her fiancé to Renee. Kevin let out a sarcastic chuckle,

"You finish? I need to know that you're finish before I speak."

"Yes. I spoke my peace."

In a truly commanding voice Kevin responded to Amanda's plea,

"I'm gonna talk low because I don't want to get loud and alarm my child. Have you lost your motherfucking mind? I don't know if you remember but I remember it like it was yesterday. You, you Amanda! Abandoned our daughter at the age of 2! She was just a baby! She didn't know what was going on and couldn't realize that her own mother left her because she couldn't handle having a special needs child. You were so wrapped up in you living your best life that the one person that supposed to mean everything to you was left behind. I can't believe you had the audacity to come to my house with this bullshit. With every breath in my being, I will do whatever it takes to keep you away from my daughter. See you don't understand, I love her more than I love my damn self. So, I need you to leave us alone, something you should be use to and never darken my doorstep again. Please get out."

Amanda gathered her things, put her raincoat back on and made her way to the front door but before turning the doorknob she informed Kevin that he would be hearing from her lawyers about Renee.

Semaj had just finished with a client when he got a call from an unknown number, to his cell. Like most people, he ignored it the first time, but the same number called right back, and Semaj figured it was a potential client. When he answered a sweet sounding, female was on the other end asking to speak to Spice, right then he knew it had to be a client. The young woman began to tell Semaj that her employer wanted to schedule a consultation with him for tomorrow and was wondering when he would be available. The conversation was pretty normal, but the young woman never mentioned the name of the person she was talking about so Semaj had to ask. The phone went silent for a moment until a loud speaking gentleman got on the phone,

"Nigga, you gone do my tatt or what? I want some big ass titties on my right forearm, so every time I shake somebody's hand they bounce. Ya heard me."

"Nigga what?", replied a confused Semaj.

He had heard of some weird request and titties on the forearm was one of the strangest but then the guy on the other end started laughing.

"My bad cuz, this Khori. I couldn't help it, you were all professional and shit on the phone. What's good with ya", laughed Khori.

The two laughed on the phone catching up with one another. Khori told his little cousin that he was in town and wanted to hook up with him later on after visiting with the family. Semaj was pleased that his cousin had finally came back after being gone for so long and asked if he had heard about their grandmother Delores. Khori had told him that she was the main reason he had made the trip from Colorado. Semaj wanted to ask his cousin why he felt he had to disappear but didn't want to spoil the reunion. He understood everybody had their own way of grieving that they had to go through after Ronnisha's passing, especially Khori because of so much that was on his heart at the time. The two talked a little while longer and Khori told Semaj he would be over to the tattoo shop later that afternoon after going see his mother Shalay but wanted Semaj to keep his presence a secret for now. Semaj agreed and they ended their call as the tattoo artist began to get his things together to close up his shop for the night. He had early morning classes to attend but couldn't wait to see his older cousin Khori. Semaj didn't only run his own tattoo shop but was going to college to better his business management skills to better his business. He learned from watching his uncle Kareem and his aunt Shalay that running a productive business sometimes took more than just the drive to do it. Semaj headed home thinking about how excited everyone will be when they find out that Khori's back in town.

Cedric was sitting in the den, with all the lights off, a glass of tequila on the rocks in his hand, listening to the rain tap against the large bay window when Sherell walked up and sat in his lap. She had just got their son Tre to go to sleep and now her attention was on the concerned face of her husband, who was really quiet. Cedric was second guessing himself about his mother, wondering if moving her to a senior living facility was the right thing,

"Baby she's gonna be in a strange place, with a bunch of strange people, by herself. Are we just pushing our problems off on somebody else because it feels like that's what I'm doing?"

"Don't you ever feel like that, we're doing what's best for her baby. Can you honestly say that all of us can give her the attention and treatment she truly needs? Because baby if you think you can pull it off, I'm behind you 100%. I don't want you to think that you're putting your mother away somewhere because you're not. You, Kareem and your sisters are giving her the help that she needs, that none of us are capable of giving her", replied Sherell as she held her husband.

Cedric sat there just thinking about "what if's" as Sherell tried to console Delores' eldest son when she began to tell him about the phone call she received from Denise. She went into detail about their conversation they had about the kids, Delores and even Denise's new job in Houston. It kind of took his mind off of the unpleasantries of abandoning his mother at a home. But the thought of his current wife and his ex-wife having a friendly conversation still felt a little weird sometimes. Cedric laughed a little,

"I'm surprised somebody haven't put us all on a talk show yet. Husband and wife get divorced, brother gets ex-wife's sister pregnant, ex-husband marries best friend and ex-wife, and new wife becomes besties. We one strange family."

"First off, you are ugly. We are not besties thank you very much, me and Dee just get each other. She was worried about the family and you stressing yourself out over it, like you are right now. And we're not a strange family, we just make it work", replied Sherell.

They sat in the den as the rain began to calm down and then the two brought themselves to bed for the night.

CHAPTER 5

A month has passed since Khori made his way back in the loving embrace of his mother Shalay, his first visit didn't go the way he imagined it would have. The last time he seen his mother, she couldn't look him in his eyes and Khori truly expected the same response. The appearance of her oldest son on her doorstep was the exact thing both of them needed. When Shalay opened the door that morning she was expecting to see anything but Khori and when her eyes fell on his face the tears of joy flooded her. She snatched him in her arms, holding onto him for dear life as she cried in his chest,

"You are really here. I thought I would never see you again baby. You are really here."

"Mama, I'm sorry"

Shalay put her finger over his lips,

"We all did what we had to do to get over some troubling times. I'm just happy that you're back."

Now that Khori has returned back to the fold he invested himself into helping the family with his grandmother Delores. He sent Erica back to make sure his company runs without a snag and Khori's lover reluctantly went back to Colorado but made it clear that she will return. Shalay was amazed at the man Khori had become and loved the fact that her son accepted Kevin being more than just a business partner in her life. Khori was blown away at how big his little brother Zach and two little sisters got over the years but when he met Kevin's daughter Renee, he could see why everybody loved her so much. Renee was a bundle of questions when she would talk to Khori and for some reason the two connected so well that it was as if they been knowing each other forever. Khori found the following everywhere little sister he lost years ago in Renee and he loved every bit of it. He made sure to include his little sisters Shantee and Lenelle anytime he went on an outing, along with his brother Zachariah. Zach thought it was the coolest thing ever that his big brother was the dope man but Khori had to constantly tell him that his business was all legit. Khori would fly his siblings to Colorado on the weekends to see what he actually does at his company; he even had his driver bring them to school when he was in town. It was as if he had never left, Shalay truly was overwhelmed that she had all of her kids back with her.

Devin touched down in New Orleans with his team for the upcoming football game and the first thing on his mind was going see his grandmother. He talked to Semaj about all of Delores' grandkids getting together to visit her all at once, Devin figured it would be good for her to see all of them. Semaj relayed the message to Khori who has been diligent at working with Dr. Jackson on CBD oil treatments for the residents at the senior facility. Once Khori found out that there were studies proving that CBD helps with Alzheimer's patients, he was determined to do whatever it took. Khori flew back and forth from his cannabis ranch in Colorado to Dr. Jackson in New Orleans, trying different strains of oils. He and Erica were just getting back in town when Semaj told him about meeting up by his grandma

Delores. Devin knew he had a game in a couple of days but connecting with his family held precedents over everything. He had a lot on his mind and one thing that always brought him back in focus was going to the gym. Devin left his hotel as he went to a nearby gym to work out and the first thing he hears is,

"Double D! That's you?"

It was his old college teammate Ricky Boyd who played the same position as him at Texas A&M. Ricky didn't make it to the league like Devin did, but he did play a few seasons in the CFL before making a career as a bouncer and personal trainer. Just like Devin, he was a mountain of a man with muscles from top to bottom but a gentle giant. Devin hadn't seen Ricky since graduation and the two started catching up on old times, but the popular defensive end's face started to attract fans from the gym. They attempted to get a few workouts in together, but Ricky had to leave and invited Devin to a strip club he bounce at while Devin's in town. After getting some stress off his chest in the gym Devin surprised his mother Alonna at work with two dozen red roses and a lunch date. He never realized how much he missed being home until he was in the city enjoying all the southern hospitality, he didn't get anywhere else. Alonna was having a proud mama moment as people walked up to her son asking for autographs and selfies with him. They enjoyed each other's company until it was time for Alonna to head back to work and Devin had to get back to the hotel for a team meeting.

"I'm a see you later for dinner, right? You know Steven gotta show off his new grill, that man is gonna barbecue us to death", stated Alonna.

Devin laughed as he told his mother he will be sure to be home for dinner.

Kevin was at his desk when he received a call from the security desk that he had a visitor waiting for him. When he got downstairs to the front of the building, he seen Amanda patiently waiting with two other men. Amanda stood back as one gentleman walked up to Kevin,

"Good afternoon Mr. Talport, my name is Joseph Rodriguez and I'm Ms. LeBlanc's attorney. I'm here to inform you that Ms. LeBlanc and myself will be pushing forward with custodial rights of Renee Talport."

"I'm a tell you like I told her the night she showed up to my house unannounced. The only way she will ever get close to my daughter is if I'm 6 feet under", replied Kevin.

Amanda's fiancé, Alex Rideau, walked up with his hand extended out to shake Kevin's hand when he explained to the agitated father who he was and that they were there only to reunite a mother to her daughter. Kevin looked at Alex with disgust in his eyes as he looked down at the stretched open hand gesture that slowly went back by Alex's side after Kevin refused to touch it. Kevin was boiling inside but he held his composure as he looked over to a smirking Amanda who had nothing to say to him. The lawyer continued to speak his peace as the words fell on Kevin's deaf ear because he was completely focused on protecting his daughter from these people standing in front of him. After her attorney finished talking, Amanda walked up,

"I tried to keep the courts out of our business, handle this like two adults but you wanted to do it the hard way and now you're forcing me to get rough with you."

"Girl the only thing you ever did rough in your life was give head. Hey Alex! She still uses two hands and too much teeth or did you teach her better", asked a sarcastic Kevin.

He snatched the paperwork from the lawyer's hand and went to the elevators to get back to his office. Once the elevator doors closed, Kevin immediately got on the phone with his family attorney to go over the procedures he needs to take to keep Renee safe from Amanda's grasp. Kevin's attorney already knew about the custody case because Amanda's lawyer already had a courier drop off a copy of the documents. It literally scared him to think that Amanda could possibly get partial or even full custody of his daughter after not being there for 14 years of her life. Kevin's lawyer assured him that his legal team will do everything possible to keep Amanda from getting full custody of Renee but because she is the biological mother of Renee, he couldn't guarantee she wouldn't get partial custody. That was something Kevin just couldn't accept, and he needed some kind of leverage, he just didn't know what. Cedric walked in his friend's office to go over some spreadsheets when he could see Kevin was going through something serious. Kevin's buddy sat in front of the office desk, put the paperwork he had off to the side and remained completely quiet. Kevin was oblivious to Cedric sitting in front of him but then he looked up,

"Damn bro, how long you been sitting there?"

"Not long, you good? Look like whatever is on that paper is fucking with you for real", replied Cedric.

Kevin told him what happened a few minutes ago and Cedric could see the pain in his friend's face. In an attempt to get his mind off of the present, Kevin asked about Cedric's mother and how she's doing at her new place. Cedric explained that it's touch and go right now but for the most part his mother is accepting her new surroundings. Cedric's best friend assured him that Delores would be perfectly fine and become very comfortable in her new home. Kevin put the legal papers to the side and let his friend know how much he appreciated their talk as he focused on the workload sitting in front of him. Cedric chuckled as he made his way out of Kevin's office,

"We could skip this whole custody shit and just get Shalay to whip her ass, you know she would do it for you."

"Get out", laughed Kevin.

Semaj was at his shop waiting on a client to show up for a new tattoo for her 21st birthday, that one of his classmates set up. Semaj been knowing Keisha since his freshman year at The University of New Orleans, and she admired his talents as an artist. She always told him that she was going to get him to do a tattoo on her one day and Keisha finally committed. Keisha Warren was a complete character, always cracking jokes and a joy to be around every time. When she called to let him know that they were on the way with the birthday girl Stephanie, Semaj found out that another one of Keisha's friends was coming also, a very sexy exotic dancer by the name of Diamond. Diamond was the epitome of attractive in Semaj's eyes, sexy, smart, confident and a fan of his tattoos. They followed each other on social media and even slid in the other's DM but in the small city of New Orleans never came face to face. Semaj was sitting in his studio, in the back of the shop, when he could hear his receptionist talking to some customers. A boisterous female blurted out behind him,

"Getcho ass up and greet me negro."

"Ain't nobody but Keisha Warren loud ass", laughed Semaj as he turned around.

He hugged Keisha as she walked up to him and glanced over at the two extremely attractive women that was with her. Not that Keisha wasn't well put together like fine wine but the other two held a caliber of sensuousness Semaj adored and besides he looked at Keisha as just a home girl. He recognized Diamond instantly as she smiled at him,

"Keisha, he is too cute."

"Girl that nigga ain't shit", replied Keisha as she pushed Semaj like he was her brother.

Semaj walked up and shook the nervous friend's hand as he asked,

"So, you must be the birthday girl?"

"Yes, I'm Stephanie. Nice to meet you. Your artwork is amazing", responded the birthday girl.

Semaj got right to business and had Stephanie tell him what she wanted her next tattoo to look like. As Stephanie began to describe her image, Semaj took out his drawing pad and started sketching out every detail she specified. Diamond was admiring all the artwork he had on the walls when she walked up behind Semaj and asked him about his nickname,

"How did you come up with the name Spice? You a cook on the side or something?"

"When I was just starting out, my friends would always say my drawings were fiya. My mentor started calling me Spice, so I stayed with it", replied Semaj.

He was trying his best not to melt into putty around Diamond, but she smelled so good and her smile literally cut through him with ease. Semaj finished the sketch of a Lotus flower Stephanie wanted as her tattoo and showed her, the birthday girl couldn't believe how he created her idea on paper. Stephanie asked him would he be able to recreate it on her and Semaj laughed,

"Girl I could tatt this in the middle of your ass cheeks and they would call this a masterpiece, I'm that good."

He closed the door to his studio, so that they could have some privacy because Stephanie's new tattoo was going to be in the middle of her breasts, and she had to take her top completely off. Semaj was preparing his equipment while the girls were talking about what she was going to get tatted and he heard one of them say,

"Damn Steph, you got some nice ass titties."

The tattoo artist laughed to himself at the remark and thought nothing of it because he has seen numerous breasts in his field of work but when Semaj turned around, he couldn't help to agree,

"You ain't never lying."

Cedric went to visit his mother after he got off work and the smile he seen on her face when he got there was all he needed to see. Delores was relaxing in the atrium of the facility that had a number of mature citrus trees, Japanese topiary, large bonsai and several types of Palm trees. The atrium even had an artificial stream that constantly flowed through the entire structure, it had a complete calming to the area. Cedric sat down next to his mother at a bench as he interlocked his fingers into hers,

"How are you doing today lady?"

His mother began to tell him how she really enjoyed the lunch they made for her, but Delores started to ask when will she be able to move back in her house. The Daniels kids used the remodeling of their mother's kitchen and the fact that Delores needed her own space as the excuse to her moving in the senior living facility. She remembered there was a fire but couldn't recall how it happened or how long she's been living at the senior home. Cedric noticed his aging mother was dressed in a thick sweater, a pair of cotton shorts and some fuzzy house slippers. He tried to brush off the comments about Delores wanting to move back home but she pushed the issue more and more. Cedric's mother began to get aggravated with him not addressing her request to move back to her home when she got up off the bench to leave. He reached out for her hand,

"Mama, where are you going?"

"Back to the room y'all shoved me in", responded a now upset Delores.

Cedric followed behind her as she stormed through the hallway trying to find her room, mumbling to herself angrily. Cedric could hear his mother make statements that her children think she's going crazy and the disrespectful way they left her in an old folks' home. Passing nurses attempted to help her but Delores shewed them away as Cedric apologized constantly for his mother's actions. He could notice his mother was getting a little turned around in the halls as she looked up and down for her room,

"Mama, you want me to bring you to your room?"

"No", shouted Delores as she walked off.

It scared him a little because Cedric seen that his mother passed her room twice, which had her name printed on a label on the door and he thought to himself what if she was alone. His mother wandered up the hallway, tugging at her sweater as she looked down the hall, with Cedric close behind her. A smiling kind nurse walked on the side of Delores and started holding a conversation with her about her kids, as they strolled down the hallway. The nurse finally made it to Delores' room and the now tired elderly mother walked in to unwind with a cup of tea the nurse had for her. After closing the door, the nurse walked up to Cedric and introduced herself, her voice had an appeasing effect as she spoke,

"Hi, she can be a handful some days, but your mother is an absolute delight to talk to. She loves talking about you, Kareem and the twins, oh don't mention the grand babies. Oh, my goodness. Sometimes she gets a little lost in these halls after her afternoon walks and I usually just walk with her to her room. It's all part of the process, with this being a new environment to her and all, they tend to get a little agitated."

Cedric was completely drained after the small scene with his mother, not knowing what to do or how to help but he thanked the nurse for stepping in when she did. He truly understood what Dr. Jackson was talking about when he said that it would get rough sometimes. Cedric thanked the nurse again and headed home for the day.

CHAPTER 6

Kareem had just made it home when he seen that his nephew Khori came over to visit with his girlfriend Erica and his mother Shalay. The site of his nephew was a joy to see, Kareem still couldn't believe the little boy that would play in the mud of his grandmother's flowerbed is now a thriving businessman and entrepreneur. Little Camille darted straight for her daddy as soon as she seen her father open the front door,

"That's my daddy! That's my daddy! Mommy daddy's home!"

"Girl everybody sees yo ugly daddy's home", responded Yolanda as she walked up and kissed Kareem.

Shalay laughed at how the toddler stood there with her hands on her hips, mad at her mother's remarks about her father. Dressed in her rainbow-colored tutu skirt and princess crown, Camille jumped in Kareem's arms as he sat in the den with his visitors. Khori had come over to tell Kareem that he purchased a suite for Devin's game Sunday against the home team and that a driver will come pick up the family. Kareem smiled as he commented,

"Oh, you balling balling neph."

"Nah unk, just wanna show the fam a good time and enjoy the game with y'all", replied Khori.

Shalay started telling Kareem about the phone call she had with Cedric about their mother, the event kind of had her teary-eyed. Khori assured his mother that the oils he sent to Dr. Jackson will help,

"Mama the test we did on the last batch really showed good improvements with slowing down the progression of the disease. I just wish I started her on it earlier, so dry them eyes."

Kareem knew his nephew was crazy smart, but he didn't know how intelligent he really was as he asked him how do they get Delores to take the new medicine. Erica chimed in the conversation as she explained the CBD oil infused tea that they created for the entire senior living facility and that Delores has an endless supply of it. Once the conversation started on anything cannabis, Khori was all about educating anyone that wanted to listen and Kareem along with Yolanda was all ears. He told them about different types, strains and all the medical factors of them until Erica had to slow him down as she laughed,

"Baby you giving them a Marijuana overload."

The small family group chilled the rest of the day enjoying each other's company as Yolanda finished cooking dinner for everyone with Shalay's help. Little Camille entertained everyone with her made-up dance routines and silly antics as she ran around the house.

After he had finished the girls' tatts, Diamond invited Semaj to meet them at The Rabbit Hole Gentleman's Club for some drinks. He happily agreed to meet them there, so that he could get another opportunity to get close to the sexy Diamond. Semaj called his brother Devin to see if he wanted to join him,

"Dude, this Diamond chick is everything. She. Is. The. One. She could be the next Mrs. Daniels. Plus, the other two fine as hell too."

"I would lil bro, but we have a curfew, remember I have a game tomorrow", responded Devin.

Caught up in all the excitement of going hang with his Internet crush, Semaj forgot his big brother had a football game the next day. Devin told him that he still wants all the grandkids to go see their grandmother after the game and Semaj agreed, telling him he told everyone. He ended the call with his big brother and headed out to meet Diamond at the strip club. It didn't take Semaj long to get to the club from his shop and the first thing he sees is two towers standing at the front door that resembled bouncers. He talked to one guy, to find out he was the friend his brother Devin told him about and Ricky let Semaj in free of charge. As soon as the double doors opened to the club the music from the sound system met Semaj's ears and the strobe lights danced to the beat as the exotic dancers did also. He glanced over the crowd and caught a glimpse of Diamond walking the birthday girl Stephanie to the main stage. Semaj found Keisha waiting at the bar as they watched all the dancers strip for Stephanie on her birthday. Because Stephanie was a waitress at the gentleman's club, it was a tradition that the dancers perform on stage with any employee on their birthday as a present. Semaj and his classmate laughed and cheered as Stephanie joined in with the dancers, as she performed a strip tease of her own. Keisha was ecstatic that her shy friend had the balls to get on stage and strip, but Semaj's eyes were focused completely on Diamond as the girls walked off the stage. The two classmates waited at the bar enjoying a few drinks when Diamond and Stephanie joined them. Semaj commended the birthday girl on her talents,

"Steph, you looked like a professional up there. You been practicing?"

"No, I've just been watching the girls every night I'm at work and tried it out for the first time", replied Stephanie.

They all had a few birthday tequila shots and Stephanie was ready to call it a night when Semaj asked Diamond if she wanted to go catch a bite to eat. The group headed out the exit doors as they ran into the bouncers waiting out front, mostly everybody stopped to talk but Stephanie made a beeline to her car across the street. The bouncers were asking Diamond where they all were headed when a loud bang, like a cannon, startled everyone to ducking for cover, Semaj hovered over Keisha and Diamond. He looked up to see a man dead in the middle of the street, Stephanie standing next to her car and two hooded dark figures standing over another man. One of the hooded figures was viciously beating the man with a baseball bat for what felt like 5 minutes and then they ran off. After the two dark figures disappeared in the night, Semaj helped the girls up off the ground and one of the bouncers ran over to check on the friend still froze standing next to her car. Keisha screamed when she seen one of the men in the middle of the street was shot in the head and Semaj immediately shielded Diamond away from the scene. The gun shot along with the frightful screams brought a crowd out front of the strip club and Semaj escorted the girls back into the building as the manager walked them to his office. Diamond was literally shaking as she buried her head in

Semaj's chest while he tried to console her and a crying Keisha who kept replaying the image in her head,

"They just shot him. They shot him down like a dog."

Semaj couldn't believe what just took place right in front of him and it all brought back some very bad memories of his little cousin Ronnisha. They all sat in the office trying to gather themselves when an NOPD officer walked in for some questions. The officer was talking with Stephanie about what happened because she was the closest to the scene, Semaj could see she was still shaken over the incident and her shirt held blood stains on it from the victim. Keisha wanted so desperately to just leave, and Diamond was in agreement with her as Semaj held both of their hands. He knew from experience that the process, as uncomfortable as it is, was necessary for the police officers to get vital information from the witnesses. The questioning was finished, and the group was allowed to leave when Diamond had a request for Semaj,

"I know you probably want to go home and forget about how this night ended but I really don't want to be alone tonight."

"Where you wanna go", asked Semaj.

Delores woke up in a cold sweat, immediately got out of her bed as she grabbed her robe and walked out of her room. The elderly mother strolled up the long hallway like it was mid-day but in actuality it was one in the morning and she made her way pass the nurse's station without one person noticing her. Delores made it to the

other side of the living quarters of the facility before
anyone seen her walking the halls and when they asked her
what she was doing the lovable senior citizen ran as fast as
her legs could take her. It was a night shift orderly that seen
Delores wandering the halls and her attempt to escape him
was halted by the stumble of her feet getting caught up in
her robe. The senior citizen fell abruptly, hitting her head
on the tile floor, the staff member helped Delores to her
feet and the flustered senior swatted at his hands, gesturing
for him to leave her alone. The orderly knew he couldn't
allow Delores to continue down the hallway, so he escorted
her to the nearest nurse's station to assist him in getting her
to her room. When the night nurse seen the upset elderly
woman, she tried her best to calm her down, but Delores
insisted that they leave her be, shouting at them that she
was just trying to get home. The concerned caretaker
attempted to talk with her patient, but Delores didn't want
anyone near her as she looked confused of her
surroundings. The nurse's only option was to give Delores
a sedative to calm her down as the orderly and herself
walked the elderly mother back to her room. The
medication did its job at working quickly because Delores
fell asleep, and the orderly was forced to carry her to her
bed. The nurse assessed the damage to Delores' forehead
because of her fall and bandaged the small bruise and
stayed with her for the rest of the night, as she wrote her
report of the incident. It wasn't the first time Delores ever
roamed the halls, but it was the first time she ever did it late
at night or injured herself doing it and the nurse knew that
Dr. Jackson needed to know, as well as her family. The
worried orderly ever so often came to check on the nurse
watching over Delores to make sure everything was okay
because he felt bad that the patient fell in front of him.

Delores seemed to have that effect on people, that they instantly care about her and the night orderly was no different as he found himself sitting with the nurse that night.

Kevin couldn't sleep thinking about the custody battle he was about to face with Amanda and Shalay could see something was truly bothering him when she woke to him not in the bed with her. She spent the night with Kevin for some quality time because they both have been extremely busy with work and family issues of their own. Kevin was sitting at the island in his kitchen with a small drinking glass of scotch on the rocks in front of him, along with the papers he received from Amanda's lawyer. He looked up at Shalay standing across the granite countertop from him,

"I'm sorry baby, I just couldn't sleep. This shit really got me all fucked up, she trying to take my baby."

"It's ok, I probably would be the same way if someone gave me some papers saying they want to have custody of my child and never been in their life", replied Shalay.

Kevin told her that his family's attorney is fighting for him to keep full custody, but the main concern of Renee's father isn't the custody battle. He doesn't want to confuse his innocent daughter about her biological mother just popping up as a stranger wanting to be a part of her life now. Shalay knew Kevin was an amazing father and only heard a piece of what Amanda was like when they were together but was just as confused as to why all of a sudden, the estranged mother wants to be in Renee's life. She did what any loving partner would do and that's just be there for her man as he vented his concerns to her. Kevin jokingly told Shalay what her brother said earlier at work. Shalay responded with a smile,

"I haven't had a fight in a while but I'm not against beating her ass behind my baby Renee."

The comment brought a smile to Kevin's face as he sipped from his glass, but the problem was staring him in the face in the form of a custody lawsuit. Shalay tried to brighten his spirits about everybody going to the game and how Khori somehow purchased a whole suite for the family. Kevin was really pleased that Shalay was able to mend the bond between her and Khori because he knew the pain his lover was going through missing her oldest child. Shalay would bury herself into her work trying to block out the fact that she didn't know where or how her son was, if he was safe or if he was hurt. The moment she reconnected with him was an instant bright light for her and she's been basking it in ever since. Kevin admired the mother that Shalay was and how she took to Renee without a glitch, right along with her beautiful children. Kevin was always nervous around other people with his daughter because he didn't know how or if they would accept her. When Renee was a toddler, Mardi Gras parades were out of the question because crowds or loud noises would set her in a frightened frenzy and most of the time Kevin was the only one that was able to calm her. Now Renee loves to meet new people and her favorite place to walk is through the mall, but Kevin still protects her at all cost. The situation he's going to battle with is no different to him now because he knows the only thing that matters to him is Renee's wellbeing and

Shalay feels the same way. Kevin put the papers away for the night as he and Shalay went back to bed. He wrapped his arms around his woman, laid his head onto her soft breast and right before falling asleep he told her,

"I love you so much, thank you for being here."

After leaving the club, Semaj followed Diamond and her friends to The Bienville Hotel where the birthday girl Stephanie had rented a room earlier for the ending of her birthday celebration. The only thing was no one was in a celebratory mood at the moment because the room was eerily quiet. Semaj sat on a sofa close to the door because he really was just ready to call it a night, after making sure the girls got in safe, but his plans were redirected when Diamond came sat next to him. She got really close, shoulder to shoulder and nudged him,

"I really didn't think our first date would start off like this, you gone have to do better."

"Ummm, ma'am most first dates start off with some flowers or candy. Not a police investigation", responded Semaj.

Diamond released a little smile at his joke as she leaned on Semaj and locked her fingers with his, but the close encounter was interrupted when Keisha plopped herself right between them. Right along with Semaj, Stephanie's boyfriend followed them to the hotel and Keisha was giving them some privacy in the other room. She was the third wheel sitting in the middle of Semaj and Diamond when she laughed,

"I am here as a human contraceptive. Spice I will not allow Diamond to take advantage of you."

"But what if I want her to take advantage of me, I'm just saying", replied Semaj.

Keisha looked at Semaj with a devilish grin as she responded,

"Just nasty, lemme see y'all kiss then."

"What!"

Diamond laughed as she shook her head at the comical Keisha who was waiting to see a passionate interaction between the couple. The trio was trying to forget the bloody incident that took place in front of them an hour ago as they talked about everything that happened that day, except the ending. Diamond asked Semaj what the craziest tattoo was he ever did for a client,

"Like the weirdest ever. Like you can't believe they want this on their body permanently."

"That's easy", laughed Semaj as he began his story.

He started telling them about a couple that came in and wanted the other's name on them, the only thing was they wanted the names tatted on their private area. Keisha burst out in laughter while Diamond was all ears as Semaj told them it was the most uncomfortable moment of his life holding another man's dick. The girlfriend wanted her name in bold italic lettering along the side of his manhood with the date they started dating on the other side. The boyfriend stated he wanted his name right above her clitoris with a single rose on each side of her pussy lips. Diamond flinched and grabbed hold of herself as she imagined the pain of a tattoo needle that close to her precious vagina,

"I know you fucking lying."

Semaj chuckled when he said he had to stop a few times because the girl kept having orgasms because of the vibration of the tattoo gun. Keisha asked if the guy was hard when he got tattooed and Semaj's response had her laughing more when he stated,

"No! Thank goodness, cause I don't know if I could have finished if he was hard in my hand."

The girls were weak laughing at Semaj's stories as it took their minds off the gruesome event that took place earlier. Semaj found himself seeing more and more attractiveness in Diamond than just the physical as they talked about school and business. Diamond told him of her aspirations to start her own dance studio after she graduate. Semaj admired the fact that she was able to see pass just being an exotic dancer and making a career of her talent. The two seemed to focus completely on one another as Keisha faded away from the conversation to a nearby sofa and fell asleep. Semaj and Diamond talked about family, friends, school, work and whatever else popped in their heads til the sun started to rise. Knowing he had a full day coming up with his brother's game, Semaj reluctantly told his sexy company he had to go home to get some rest and smitten Diamond understood. She walked him to the door and Semaj asked her,

"Would it be out of line to kiss you right now?"

"It would be completely out of line if you don't kiss me right now", replied Diamond.

CHAPTER 7

Alonna was with Dashanae putting on Devin's jerseys, both of them were getting ready for the game. Steven, on the other hand, been ready for the game since eight that morning and was pacing around like he was actually playing,

"Y'all just now getting ready? Always my beautiful girls keeping us late."

"Daddy don't do us like that. Besides, it's just 10 and the game don't start until 12", replied Dashanae.

Alonna looked at her husband in complete agreement with her daughter as she told Steven to go call Semaj, to make sure he's getting ready. No one knew about or heard the news of the fatal assault that took place right in front of Semaj the night before. He had been home a few hours, taking a nap after leaving Diamond at the hotel, when Steven called him,

"Bruh, I know you not sleep. Boy if you don't get dressed and get over here."

"I'm on my way now", replied Semaj as he jumped out of bed and rushed to his mother's house.

In between running through his apartment putting on clothes, Semaj noticed he got a text from Diamond that just read,

"I really enjoyed our talk."

He couldn't do anything but smile at the fact that she reached out first because he was on her mind, but Semaj couldn't deny the realization that the precious gem he spent the night with was embedded in his thoughts. The idea of starting a closer relationship with her began to sound very appealing to him as he replied to her text with the same response. Semaj was almost to his mother's house when Khori called him about getting together after the game, just all their cousins, to go visit their grandmother. In all the things that happened last night Semaj forgot they were supposed to get together to surprise Delores with a visit. He agreed to meet Khori at the senior home as he pulled up to his mother's driveway and the limo bus arrived right behind him. Steven darted out the front door of the house as Cedric stepped off the bus,

"Let's get it people! Time for some football."

"Damn, I knew Khori was sending us in style, but this thing is nice nice", replied Steven.

Semaj along with his crew got on the party bus with the rest of the Daniels and they made their way to the Dome to enjoy the game.

Kevin and Renee were visiting his parents' home on St. Charles Ave/Garden district for the day when his father pulled him outside to have a man to man talk about the situation his in. Martin Talport was a no-nonsense businessman, if it didn't make money it didn't make sense to him but his granddaughter Renee was his everything next to his own son. When he got word, that Amanda LeBlanc was trying for custody rights for Renee, Martin wasn't having it at all and began talking with private investigators. Kevin sat in his family's plush immaculate backyard with his father, who had a manila folder in front of him and listened attentively as his father spoke. Martin informed Kevin about everything Amanda had been doing since she left New Orleans 14 years ago, but the key info was her fiancé Alex Rideau who was an advocate for special needs children and the foundations he support. Alex was a top tier businessman in Las Vegas, that was testing the waters out in the Crescent City with a powerful business deal with an upcoming casino boat. Being that one of Alex's biggest foundations is working with special needs, the hired investigators figured it would look strange that his wife to be abandoned her own child with special needs and that's the reason for the sudden custody battle Kevin found himself in. The more he thought about it, the more pissed Kevin got,

"Sorry for the language pops but I can't believe this bitch is trying to use my kid for publicity."

"The bitch ain't getting close to my grandchild son. That motherfucker lost that right when she walked away from her", replied Kevin's father.

Martin ran it all down to Kevin that their lawyers will have a meeting Monday, to come up with some sort of agreement and try to keep it out of the courts but the info the private investigator got would stay in their back pocket for insurance. Kevin wanted it all to just be over with, but that concern went away like a slight breeze when Renee came outside with her grandmother Maxine. The two had made some homemade iced tea and Renee was so proud of the fact that she helped in making it. Martin's only grandchild happily poured him a glass of her tea as he tended to the steaks he had on the grill. Kevin watched as his daughter was engaged in a deep conversation with his father of whatever Renee was fascinated about at the time and it brought a well of tears to Kevin's eyes. The love he seen exchanged in that one moment was what Kevin desired for his baby girl all the time and the fact that Amanda was trying to disturb that scared Kevin a little. Maxine saw the single tear roll down Kevin's cheek,

"Baby there's nothing at all to worry about so wipe those tears. I wish we wouldn't have set you up with that nutcase in the first place, but I would have never gotten my beautiful Princess out of it."

"Mama, I'm just gone enjoy the day and deal with that chick when I have to", replied Kevin.

Maxine asked about Shalay and why he didn't bring her with him to the barbecue. Kevin told his mother about the game Shalay's nephew is playing in today and how the whole family is going to the Dome. He let his mother know how he and Renee was invited to join them, but he wanted to enjoy some family time with his own parents. Maxine just glowed with the idea that her son wanted to spend his Sunday with her instead of the luxury suite fun he could have had.

Dr. Jackson usually makes his visits during the week with all of his patients, but he wanted to make a special visit to his favorite patient Mrs. Delores. He knocked on her front door and the aged Queen of the Daniels family peeked out with the most delightful smile, that she brightened Dr. Jackson's day. He had become a familiar face to Delores, right along with the nurses who regularly made visits to check her vitals and make sure she's taking her medicine. Dr. Jackson's facility wasn't a very large one with 120 beds and 30 staff members, but he always made sure that every one of his patients were well taken care of under his care. He prided himself on the fact that he was able to connect to each individual on a personal level there, especially because most of his patients were losing the ability to remember their own age sometimes. Dementia and Alzheimer's disease became a long-life journey for Dr. Jackson after losing his grandmother to the same disease when he was a teen. Delores reminded him of her so much that he spent countless time just sitting with her talking. Dr. Jackson also relished in the idea that Khori took a certain interest in the well-being of his grandmother and the studies they both had a hand in would help so many more patients. Delores sat with her doctor talking about her children as they both enjoyed a cup of special brewed tea Dr. Jackson had prepared. The specialist listened as the elderly monarch recalled stories of her childhood, her marriage and her children. The conversation was going really well until Delores noticed she wasn't in her own home and suggested that she was ready to go. Just like her children had been saying to her for the past two months, Dr. Jackson told Delores that her kitchen is being remodeled and the best place for her right now is staying with him. Delores liked her doctor's kind face but couldn't recall his name so she always referred to him as baby, but the nickname had become common for anyone that came to the senior's door. Dr. Jackson noticed that the gradual decline of Delores' brain had begun to slow down but the decline was still there, and it brought a cloud to the sunlit shine he seen in her eyes. The visiting physician gathered his things as he prepared to leave for the day when Delores asked again,

"When will I be able to get back home? Cedric said I would be going home soon."

"I will check on that as soon as I get back to the office, I promise", replied Dr. Jackson.

He walked out a little down that he could see that the dreadful ailment was progressing as common symptoms began to show up in their conversation. The doctor didn't want to alarm the family, but he knew from past experiences with other patients that his sweet Mrs. Delores probably won't see her home again.

      The Daniels crew were all enjoying the luxury suite Khori got for everybody as they watched the game. Cedric had his little man Tre sitting next to him while they watched the event but the young 5- year-old was more interested in the catered food than the football game. The twins both were just amazed at how far their sons have come, with Devin becoming a professional football player and Khori a well-respected businessman. It seemed as if Alonna was cheering louder than anyone in the Dome every time Devin hit the field and Dashanae was right there with her, screaming her brother's name. Even though the whole family was in their hometown, with their home team playing, every one of the Daniels' family was rooting for Devin's team to win. Shalay remembered Erica from the funeral four years ago, the two never really got a chance to actually talk to one another and Khori's mother took the opportunity for them to get to know each other better. Erica welcomed the conversation as she sat with Shalay talking about Khori and his siblings. Khori's girlfriend was weak with laughter when she heard about his younger years,

"Bae, you didn't tell me you and Devin would run in the backyard naked."

"Mama stop it! Why you gotta bring that up again? Baby, I was a free spirit back then and I felt free with no clothes on.", replied a laughing Khori.

Erica enjoyed the time getting to know Shalay better, especially because she didn't have a mother herself and experiencing a motherly figure really felt good. She glanced over the family and was pleased to see strong women that could hold their own but let their men lead, a quality that was lost a long time ago. Erica watched as Sherell made sure Cedric was comfortable watching the game, if he needed another drink or something to eat and he always thanking her with a kiss of gratitude. She smiled seeing Alonna rave about her son's athletic feats on the field and Steven standing there like the proudest of fathers, as they both enjoyed watching him. Yolanda was the mode Erica geared to be, her presence simply exuding royalty but she carried a demeanor of being a caring lover to Kareem and the heartwarming spirit of a protective mother to Camille. Khori could see his woman was enjoying the time with his family and the smile his little cousin Camille brought to her face every time she bounced around,

"You not catching baby fever, are you?"

"Boy stop it. You are enough child for me right now", replied Erica.

The only thing was she actually adore the idea of her own bundle of joy but before she could express the notion to Khori the sounds of Alonna shouting Devin's name caught everyone's attention. The whole family was looking on the field as Devin laid on the ground holding his left arm in pain. The star player broke his forearm on a tackle and was being escorted off the field to the tunnel that lead to the locker room. Alonna could see the pain her son was in as he walked off and she darted out the suite to be by his side with Steven right behind her. Once the field had cleared of the medical staff and the game continued, the lively spirit of the Daniels' suite slowly dropped as everyone worried about Devin. Semaj sat there with a concerned Dashanae, waiting to hear any news from their mother about their brother. The rest of the family started to gather their things to leave because no one wanted to watch the game after Devin's accident. It was a quiet ride back home for Shalay and her crew, as she got the news from Alonna that her nephew severely broke his arm during a tackle.

After checking on his brother's injuries, Semaj found himself standing in front of the Tulane Medical Center wondering what he was going to do next. He didn't have any appointments at the shop, and he wasn't in the mood to just sit at home doing nothing. Alonna was not moving from Devin's side at the hospital and Steven brought Dashanae home after they got the news that the football injury wasn't really that serious. Semaj did one thing he hadn't done in a long time and that's just relax while he cruises the city, sightseeing. Getting his tattoo shop off the ground kept Semaj on a constant run, never really getting a chance to enjoy the spoils of his hard work and today turned out to be the perfect opportunity to do just that. It had been so long since Semaj drove up Canal Street that it looked strange and new to him. He was stopped at the corner of Canal and Elk Place when he noticed the newly remodeled Joy Theatre had finally opened its doors again. Semaj never been to the Joy but heard stories from his grandmother about when she was young and the history of the theatrical landmark. He thought about going in to see what all the fuss was about over the renovated antique, but a phone call erased that idea as soon as he seen who it was. Diamond's smiling voice came through as she asked Semaj what he was doing at the moment. When he told her, he was "playing tourist" for the day, Diamond invited herself and Semaj had no problem at all with her tagging along. She told him where her apartment was, and Semaj raced to get to her. He pulled up to her apartment complex on Elysian Fields and wasn't expecting the girl next door image that walked up to his car. The scent of honey jasmine intoxicated Semaj as soon as Diamond sat in the front seat, but her perfume was overpowered by the pure visual. Her sundress draped over her exquisite athletic body frame like fine silk as she sat with her legs completely crossed revealing her smooth cocoa butter glazed skin. Semaj didn't know if he wanted to grope, grab or kiss her as Diamond sat there with the most innocent of faces. He thought about just driving to Lake Ponchartrain but because it was a Sunday Semaj knew it would be crowded,

"So, where you wanna go first, Missy?"

"I'm following your lead, wherever you wanna take me", replied Diamond.

Semaj was concerned about Diamond's friend and asked about her as they made their way to their destination.

"She's holding up good, better than I could imagine or she's putting up a good front", responded Diamond.

Semaj figured the French Market would be a nice spot for them to visit and then he could take her to the Riverwalk afterwards. He tried his best to focus on the road, but Diamond's presence was just too appealing not to stare at. They talked about what they wanted to do after graduation again because Diamond's aspirations of opening a dance school really fascinated Semaj. He could see Diamond wasn't your ordinary exotic dancer that only thought about chasing the bag and taking men for their money, but she had a head on her shoulders for business. The more they talked on the ride to their destination the more attracted Semaj became to her and vice versa. Semaj parked his car a few blocks away from the market and got out to let Diamond out of the car,

"Oh, you are a true gentleman."

"My mama would beat my ass if I let a woman open her own door", laughed Semaj.

They made their way down the sidewalk, pass the Hard Rock Café and Café du Monde til they arrived at the front entrance to the French Market. There they seen a sea of vendors selling all sorts of items from fresh produce to home décor and more. Diamond held onto her date's hand as they walked through the crowd looking at handmade trinkets, souvenirs and urban craftsmanship. They didn't know what to go look at first, as one would point out one thing and the other would see something new. The two were truly enjoying themselves together, Semaj bought his date a New Orleans city skyline portrait she was eyeing, and Diamond bought him a hand carved African mask. They were heading back towards Semaj's car as they walked along the Riverwalk when they encountered two guys that recognized Diamond from the gentleman's club she works at. One of the guys was completely disrespectful reaching for Diamond's hand, trying to talk to her in front of Semaj, disregarding him completely and the other just smiling with the weirdest perverted grin. Semaj being the man that he is, stepped in front of the guy trying to talk to Diamond and told him, with the sternest of voice, that it was time for him to go. Diamond could see the encounter was about to turn into a serious altercation and took Semaj's hand to walk away, avoiding any fist being thrown. For Diamond, it was like trying to keep an agitated pit bull under control, as the couple walked off. The two guys stood on the sidewalk shouting obscenities to the both of them and Semaj turned to respond but Diamond corralled him back by standing face to face with him. She looked him in the eyes,

"I'm with you, not them, not anyone else just you. We were having a beautiful day together and I don't know about you, but I want to continue to enjoy the rest of this day, just you and me. Let's go."

With fire in his eyes Semaj listened to his date, took her hand and they made their way back to his car to leave. Semaj wanted so bad to go back to confront the two degenerates on the sidewalk, but Diamond's soft hands held him in check.

The young couple made it back to Semaj's apartment after grabbing two po-boys to grub on and watch a movie. The ambiance in the Bachelor suite gave Diamond a sense of relaxation as she made herself comfortable. Semaj wasn't the average 20-year-old that had clothes everywhere, game console plugged up to the big screen TV and liquor bottles scattered all over. His place was calm, clean and well put together with a nice afro centric flare to it. Diamond admired the vintage portraits of black leaders and artworks that covered the walls, as she looked around. Semaj walked in the living room with two glasses and a two liter of cold drink as he chuckled,

"I can't believe you really didn't want to go to a restaurant and get a bite to eat. Instead, you wanna chump down on these sandwiches and look at TV."

"I told you I'm not difficult, I like simple shit and this shrimp on French is perfect", replied Diamond as she took a bite of her sandwich.

They chilled on the sofa, going through the guide looking for something to look at on cable while they ate but the conversation kept them both occupied. They found themselves entertained with just relaxing and talking with one another as Semaj laid his head in Diamond's lap. She found herself just looking down at his face, looking at a very handsome man that isn't just looking for a quick hook-up or accomplishing a challenge of sleeping with a stripper. The attraction was there with both of them, and Semaj tried his best to restrain himself from just jumping the line, Diamond on the other hand went in for the kill as she initiated their first passionate kiss. Their lips and tongues intertwined as their bodies grew closer to one another. Semaj sat on the couch while Diamond straddled his lap with his hands clamped onto her soft round ass. His hardened manhood pressed up against her already moist juice box and the girth felt between her legs sent tingles through her body, anticipating her first encounter with it. Semaj slid the spaghetti straps of Diamond's dress off of her shoulders and her succulent caramel breast with silver dollar sized Hershey kisses areolas stared at him. He couldn't help but to trace out her nipples with his tongue, every rotation around, hardened her nipples to an ultimate sensitivity. She rotated her hips, grinding on his dick every time he sucked on her nipples and released. Semaj laid her on the sofa, as he eased her sundress off, revealing a white see-through string bikini that covered a plump desiring pussy. He reached for the delicate undergarment and slowly pulled them away from her skin as the soft sound of her lower lips made a kissing sound when she opened her legs. Semaj knew her juices were flowing and had to get a taste, so he did, and his tongue was flooded with her delectable cream as he twirled his tongue around her clit. Diamond has had some good head before, but Semaj brought her to a new height with his oral skills and she wasn't ready for it as she tried to run away. He pulled her closer, burying his head deep between her legs as his mouth engulfed her pleasure pocket and his oral appendage found itself deep inside her. She could feel his tongue slide easily in and out of her as his thumb massaged her throbbing clit. Semaj didn't know it yet, but Diamond was about to damn near drown him when she felt that tingling feeling of her first orgasm with him, and she urged him to move back. He could feel that she was getting ready to climax as he slid two fingers deep inside and devoured her clit in a circular motion, sucking on it ever so vigorously. The damn was broken, and the flood gates released as Diamond squirted off her first intense orgasm, splashing it into Semaj's face. For a split second it caught him off guard, but he quickly recovered and continued doing what he was doing as he licked the juices off her clit, while she shivered out the last of her spasm. Still trying to adjust from an incredible outburst of cream Diamond decided it was Semaj's turn to submit to her oral performance. She unbuttoned his jeans and pulled out a massive veined 10 inched piece of meat that she barely was able to wrap her hand around. She gazed at her dessert and licked the opening of the head, making the mandingo jump in her hand. Diamond went in for a better taste and the hardened snake filled her oral cavity, pushing its way to the back of her throat. She engaged an immaculate suction as she pulled back, sucking away all the built-up saliva left on his dick. Her hand stroked up and down the shaft as her fingers caressed his large helmet top. Diamond went in again, attempting to take him all in and an erotic gag emerged as his helmet pressed against the back of her throat. She wanted so much to finish the job and have him explode in her throat but her jumping pussy wanted him inside her so badly. With one last long suck, she pulled the appendage from her mouth, stood above the stiffened staff and eased down onto it. Semaj's head pushed open her lips, slid deep inside, as her juices soaked his dick's skin and her walls gripped hold of him. The pleasure sent an electrifying feeling through both of their bodies as Diamond slid up and down the massive ride that filled her. They locked eyes and a connection like they never felt before was made, as a simple fuck instantly turned into love making. Semaj pushed deeper and deeper into her as Diamond rode the wave, pushing back as she grasped him with her muscles. Everything around them seemed to disappear as his strokes brought her to another spastic orgasm and her juices dripped to his balls. He couldn't hold on anymore as he felt himself about to bust and Diamond was finally about to get her chance to finish him off. She jumped off his dick, inserted him in her mouth and she could taste herself on him as he fucked her mouth. He let out a deep moan and boom, he unloaded his thick cream filling. She stroked him as the last skeet shot in her mouth and he watched as it disappeared down her gullet, she sucked one more time to make sure it was all gone as she stroked the now flaccid meat to sleep. They laid there naked in each other's sweat, relishing the magnificent moment they both just experienced.

CHAPTER 8

It was a gloomy morning when Shalay got a call from Cedric about their mother. Delores had managed to get pass anyone that could have stopped her, and she was wandering the area. The head nurse had every orderly in the facility searching the grounds for her, but no one actually knows how long she had been gone, they just knew she was missing after breakfast. Cedric told his sister that he was on his way to the center to help look for Delores and that Kareem was already there with Alonna. Shalay wiped the sleep from her eyes, told her son Zachariah to watch his little sisters and darted out the door to assist her siblings to find their mother. The ominous clouds opened up to a down pour and worry started settling in with Shalay as she walked the streets of the neighborhood surrounding the senior living facility. With no umbrella or raincoat, Cedric walked through the rain as if it had no effect on him because he was desperate to find the wandering grandmother. The worry bug began to disable all of Delores' children as every empty street showed no sign of their mother. The rain started to come down hard, Cedric heart raced thinking that Delores is somewhere soaked to the bone and the only thing keeping everyone from seeing Cedric's tears was the rain on his face. Shalay started shouting her mother's name as she frantically searched but they all were relieved when Alonna received a call from the head nurse stating Delores was found on the porch of a nearby home. The resident was concerned that the elderly woman was lost, called the nursing home and an orderly quickly went to retrieve her. The siblings were so relieved that their mother was found safe, and a unified sigh of relief came over them all but the damage was already done. The stress level brought Cedric to his knees as he clutched his chest in pain and his siblings rushed to his aid. He laid there as he tried to catch his breath, Shalay tightly holding onto his hand, his head resting in Alonna's lap and Kareem calling 911 for assistance. The Daniels' kids were in deep and they were determined to save their brother as he laid there fading away. The sounds of an ambulance siren could be heard closing in on their location and Kareem stood in the middle of the street to guided them to the sidewalk where his sisters were with his big brother. Shalay cried for Cedric to stay with her as his eyes sat there closed while the paramedics rushed to get him on the gurney. Cedric's siblings rushed to their cars to follow the ambulance to the hospital as he was rushed to the emergency room. Alonna called Sherell to give her the bad news while Kareem was on the phone with Yolanda letting her know what was going on. As soon as Yolanda got off the phone with her man, she felt obligated to let her little sister know of Cedric's illness and Denise immediately cried out in disbelief. Even though she was taking her claim in Houston at the moment, Cedric's ex-wife decided to gather her daughter and be at the Daniels' side.

Kevin was in his office oblivious to any of the events that took place, going through his own turmoil as his court date was coming up soon and he noticed that Sherell nor Cedric was at work. He called Cedric's cell to only get the answering machine, he tried Sherell and found the same response. It wasn't like them to not answer his calls and

Kevin felt a little concerned, thinking something was wrong with his second mother, Delores Daniels. Kevin called his lover and when Shalay answered he knew something was drastically wrong because Cedric's sister could barely get her words out pass her crying voice. He finally was able to reel her in as his calming vocals lightened her stress level and she was able to tell him where they were,

"Baby, we downstairs in the waiting room of the ER."

"I'm on my way", replied Kevin as he ran out his office.

Being the employee in charge of all the medical records at Tulane Medical Center, Kevin had some perks others weren't privileged to have as he scrolled through his tablet and he quickly looked up to see why his best friend was being hospitalized. As the elevator brought him down to the first floor, he seen that the first report was that Cedric was being assessed for a mild heart attack and they were waiting on a doctor's confirmation of the emergency. As soon as Shalay seen her beau walk in the waiting room, she rushed over, wrapped her arms around him and buried her face in his chest. Kevin did his best to comfort her as he explained to the rest of the family that Cedric is under the best care and he'll get the head doctor to talk to them as soon as he has some news. The Daniels' siblings sat patiently waiting with Kevin as everybody else began to file in, like Alonna's husband Steven, Yolanda and Sherell. Sherell's face was plastered with worry and Yolanda sat next to her as they interlocked their fingers consoling one another. It was an unwanted similar feeling to Sherell as she waited to hear any good news from the doctors working on Cedric. She began to think back to when Cedric was in that horrendous car accident, that put him in a coma for 7 months and the thought of not being able to talk to her best friend again felt like a concrete boulder in her stomach. Yolanda could feel Sherell shaking in her hands and kept reassuring her that he will pull through this with flying colors just like he did before. All her questions along with concerns was about to be answered when the double doors to the ER swung open and this tiny Vietnamese doctor walked up to the family to tell them about Cedric.

Khori went over to Devin's hotel room to check on his cousin after the accident and hospital visit, he had. They didn't know about their uncle Cedric yet and were just enjoying each other's company as Devin got his things together to leave for his mother's house. He decided to stay in New Orleans while he heals up from his broken arm and get some quality time with his family. Khori got the news of their grandmother wandering out of the senior nursing home and called to make sure all was well over there. The nurses were so use to Khori calling about Delores that they assumed he was her actual family practitioner until he showed up for a visit one time. They both went to visit their grandmother as soon as they got the news but Khori and Devin wondered why neither of their parents were at the center checking on their grandmother. Delores sat in her rocking chair in her room quietly as her nurse, who was keeping a close eye on her, whispered the events to the concerned grandkids. When the little old lady caught sight of her two oldest grandsons a smile lit up her face,

"Y'all gone stand over there or y'all gone come talk to me."

"Lady, you know we here to see you and you only", smiled Devin.

Khori thanked the nurse for sitting with his grandmother as he and his cousin sat with Delores. Just seeing her two boys brought a joyous feeling to Delores as she asked them how they were doing. Devin was pleased to see the smile on his grandmother's face as she talked about her time in the senior center. Worried that she would wander away again, Khori started the ball rolling on getting Delores her own personal nurse that would stay with her during the day like a home health nurse. His grandma could see the seriousness in his face as Khori pecked away at his tablet,

"Boy what are you doing over there, all serious faced."

"Nothing mama, just taking care of some business, that's all", replied Khori.

Delores wrapped her soft aged hand around Khori's hand as she pulled it away from his electronic device and laid her other hand on his cheek. She told him that work will always be available and that he needs to sit back to enjoy his fruits. The young entrepreneur put his tablet down and just smiled at his grandmother's old school knowledge. Devin asked if anyone been over to visit and Delores' response threw Khori for a loop,

"Just you boys, ya sisters haven't been over at all. When they say identical, they mean it. All them girls do is chase behind them raggedy ass boys all day. Cedric, I'm just glad you and Kareem got y'all shit together."

Khori stood there stunned at the fact that his grandmother recognized them as her sons and when he tried to reply Devin stopped him cold. It saddened Devin that the whole

time he was sitting there talking to his grandmother she
didn't see him as her grandchild and Khori was trapped in
the same funk as his cousin. They couldn't bare seeing her
like that anymore and excused themselves, kissing her ever
so softly on the forehead as they said their goodbyes. Devin
made his way to the front door, while Khori was telling
Delores he will see her later, when he got a call from his
mother about their uncle.

Semaj woke from a restful sleep to the beautiful sight
of Diamond laying peacefully next to him under the covers
and he thought to himself how he could get this lucky. Her
smooth caramel skin tone just seemed to glow when the
light hit it and Semaj couldn't help but to kiss her. His lips
woke her as she smiled at him and quickly covered her
mouth,

"You all close to me and I know I got morning breath."

Semaj laughed as Diamond rushed to the bathroom to
freshen up and get dressed. He got out of bed, looking
through his phone and noticed a bunch of missed calls right
along with text messages. Before Semaj could call anyone
and get any kind of information, Devin was knocking on
his door,

"Hey lil bro, we gotta get to the hospital."

Semaj's big brother waited in the living room for Semaj to
get dressed, while Khori waited outside in the car.
Diamond could see Semaj rushing around getting himself
together and told him she'll leave in a cab. He stopped in
his tracks and looked at her,

"Nonsense, just sit here and relax. There's food in the fridge."

"You gone leave me in your apartment, you're really trusting."

"I believe I can trust you, especially after the two round session we had last night. Besides, I know where you go to school, where you work and where you live. Oh, and I figured you would want to redeem yourself after tapping out last night anyways", smiled Semaj.

Diamond laughed while pushing Semaj out the room and he ran off with his brother to the hospital. Being a dancer, Diamond was used to guys trying to buy her affection with money or gifts, but Semaj was different. She seen a quality in him she hadn't seen in many men she had encountered before, and it felt good to be wanted as a person and not as property. Diamond prided herself on the fact that she didn't put herself out as "everything has a price" type of female and she wore that as a badge of honor. She studied the art of seduction, in every aspect and knew she didn't have to degrade herself to get what she wanted. Diamond knew from a young age that men were visual creatures and most of the time all they wanted to do was watch, so she created that on her paid social media sites. What she didn't make in the strip clubs on stage, she made up for on her paid sites and most of the time she made more money because the videos or photos were more risqué than dancing. Diamond really liked Semaj and knew she would have to tell him about her extra money ventures soon before it came to them on the street like those two guys did on the Riverwalk. But for now, she did exactly what he told her to do and that was relax while she laid on his sofa looking at TV. His shirt laying over the armrest carried his scent and Diamond couldn't help but to smell it as it brought back some enjoyable memories of when she first met him. She remembered the long conversation she had with him that night that went on til the sun came up, the morning text that just made her smile and the walks through the market. Diamond caught herself thinking Semaj just may be the one for her but didn't want to get her feelings too into it because she didn't know if he felt the same.

"C'mon now girl, get a grip", as she laughed at herself.

After making sure his friend was okay at the hospital, Kevin made his way to a meeting he had to have with his family lawyer. Kevin's nerves were so bad that he felt sick to the stomach and it only got worse the closer he got to the lawyer's office. Fearing the fact that Amanda could possibly get partial custody of his daughter started to become a reality to him. He walked in the office and waited for the secretary to escort him to a conference room down the hall. Kevin's lawyer walked in with his team of associates, introduced themselves and instantly got to work on keeping Kevin with full custody of his daughter. The lawyers explained that the meeting they all were about to have was just a preliminary one on one so that both parties could discuss their needs without a judge, to see if they could come up with a resolution. Kevin could care less to what Amanda had to say because he didn't want Renee anywhere close to the woman that gave birth to her. He sat at the long wooden table, leg bouncing because it was the only thing keeping him calm and his lawyer reassuring to him that everything would be fine. The door to the conference room opened as the secretary walked in Amanda, Alex and their lawyer. They all sat across from one another like two teams ready for battle but the sly smirk on Amanda's face sent rage through Kevin's body as he blurted out,

"I be damn you get close to my child."

Kevin's lawyer tried to curb his client's anger as they began their talks of the situation of custody. Kevin silently listened as the two law firms went back and forth with ideas of joint custody, while Amanda taunted him with under eyed looks. He could see she was trying to get a reaction from him, trying to get him to have an outburst but Kevin restrained himself and just held onto the armrest of the chair he was sitting in as his anger bubbled inside. Amanda's lawyer told them that she wanted to have unsupervised visit that would eventually lead up to partial custody where Kevin and Amanda would alternate holidays throughout the year. Kevin didn't want Renee's estranged mother nowhere near his daughter let alone be with her unsupervised and he expressed those feelings,

"You really think I'm a let you near her? After you left her without a goodbye? Without a single explanation why? And you just wanna pop-up in her life now."

"Mr. Talport, my client understands that she has made mistakes in the past that may bring concern to you regarding your daughter but she's trying to correct those mistakes and start a new", explained Amanda's lawyer.

Kevin had had enough of the talking as he got up from the table and walked out the conference room to the exit door, Amanda's fiancé Alex chased behind him attempting to talk. The two men stood outside the lawyer's office and it was the only time Alex had a chance to express to Kevin how he really felt about the situation. He told Kevin that he understood his concerns about Amanda just showing up and demanding to be in Renee's life all of a sudden. Kevin really wasn't trying to hear anything Alex was talking about, but he listened because Kevin could see that Alex was genuine with his words.

"Say man, I respect the fact that you feel you love Amanda, and you will do whatever it takes to make her happy and just maybe that involves getting me to agree with y'all connecting with my daughter. But see my daughter is my everything, no one is more important to me than her, no one. That little girl is beyond special to me and a lot of other people. Amanda lost that privilege to experience how special Renee truly is the day she walked away from her and I will protect my baby from that hurt with my last breath", stated Kevin as he walked to his car.

CHAPTER 9

Sherell was sitting next to Cedric's hospital bed after the ER doctor explained to the whole family that Cedric had a mild heart attack, and they will keep him overnight just for observational purposes. The family was a little relieved that Cedric's condition wasn't too serious, but the doctor told them that another stressful occurrence could bring on another episode. Sherell along with the rest of the family knew why Cedric was stressing so much and like always band together to make sure it didn't happen again. After making sure their brother was okay, Cedric's siblings started to leave so that he could get some much-needed rest. Yolanda was walking down the hallway with her small family when she heard the pitter-patter of little feet shuffling towards her and her niece's voice,

"Auntie Londa, we found you."

"Hey girl, I didn't think we would've caught up to y'all", stated Denise.

Shalay and Alonna both couldn't hide the surprise on their faces as they watched their brother's ex-wife walk up to them. Denise jumped on the first flight to New Orleans as soon as she heard from her sister that Cedric was being rushed to the hospital. Denise was greeting the Daniels clan when Devin, Khori and Semaj walked up to everyone in the lobby. Khori went straight to his mother as he whispered to her,

"Mama, what the hell Denise doing here?"

"Boy, shut up", laughed Shalay as she pinched him on the shoulder.

Denise told her sister she just wanted to visit with Cedric for a minute and she would be on her way. Yolanda was just as shocked as the rest of the family because she didn't expect Denise to show up from Texas that quick. The twins wanted to stay after seeing Denise but Steven and Khori pulled them away, both telling them,

"No, we going home."

"I know they cool and all but baby, you think that's a good idea of Denise showing up like this", asked Kareem as he and Yolanda watched Denise make her way to Cedric's room.

Kareem's baby mama just kept walking to their car as she told him that they are all grown adults and that they will stay out of their business. Denise walked in the room to Sherell talking to Cedric and the surprised face met her again as little Ashley announced her arrival to the couple in the room. Sherell immediately went to Denise and hugged her because their talk earlier was a premonition of what she was experiencing at the moment. She realized Cedric's worrying diminished his health because he was too busy caring for others and not himself. Denise knew how much Delores meant to Cedric and her being placed in a nursing home would stress him out more than anything. Sherell just held onto Denise's hand, so overjoyed that she was there with her, not because of them still being friends but because Denise was a woman that understood how stubborn Cedric could be. She knew how Cedric would push himself aside for the betterment of another and disregard his life to make someone else's better. Sherell loved her in-laws to the moon and back but they didn't see the stress Cedric would put himself through to keep them happy if he could. Making sure all family situations are taken care of, if anything is needed or out of place, he would fix it and then when he comes home, he's completely drained. Sherell knew it wasn't something new with Cedric and that he has been that way since he was young but now it's taking a toll on his body. She also knew Denise would have probably been the only other person that seen the stressed side of him before because he hides it from his family. Cedric was sitting up in his bed while Ashley entertained him with her extravagant stories of Texas and their new house. Denise and Sherell just sat there smiling as they seen the light shine back in Cedric's eyes as he listened to the little bundle of joy that was Ashley. It was a sigh of relief for Sherell to see her husband bouncing back to the man she loved, and she asked Denise,

"You staying with Yolanda and Kareem while you're here?"

"Nah girl, I reserved a hotel close to the airport. One of the perks working for NASA, free rooms", replied Denise.

They all sat there a little longer visiting with Cedric until Ashley began to get a little bored of the hospital scene and Denise decided it was time for them to go. She said her goodbyes and little Ashley promised Cedric that she would see him again before she leaves to go back to Texas. Cedric smiled as he responded,

"You betta come back and see me too. Now come here and gimme kiss."

Khori made it back to his mother's house after dropping his cousins off and got on the phone with Erica to start having some of his oil treatments sent to his uncle Cedric's house. Erica brought a muc

needed smile to Khori's face when she responded,

"Mr. Daniels I'm coming back in town with this next shipment you ordered because I haven't smelled you in weeks."

"Well Ms. Pleasant that would be much appreciated because your delectable scent has escaped me and I needs that in my life", replied Khori.

The two laughed on the phone with one another as Erica gave Khori the rundown of the week's business and transactions. After a long list of cramming numbers, conference calls and working out schedules Erica told Khori she would see him in a few days when she flies back in town. Khori put his phone away and went to see what his mother was doing in the kitchen. As soon as he stepped in the kitchen he was met with a question,

"Not saying I was listening to your conversation but why don't you tell that girl you love her?"

"Mama she know that, I ain't gotta tell her that."

"If I know it or not, it's always nice to hear it from the man I have strong feelings for to tell me he loves me. That baby bends over backwards for you. A simple, I love you goes a long way, I'm just saying baby", replied Shalay.

Khori just smiled as he helped his mother put away some dishes and his little sister Lenelle walked in asking Shalay if Renee would be coming over. The whole scary situation with Cedric being in the hospital made Shalay forgetful of the issues Kevin was dealing with himself. She rushed to call him after telling Lenelle she would try to go pick Renee up later. Kevin's phone kept going straight to voice mail after three tries and Shalay finally just decided to leave a message,

"Hey baby, I was just calling to check on you. I know you had that meeting today and I was just making sure everything was okay. Gimme a call later, love you. Oh, and Lenelle really wants to see Renee today, she keeps asking about her. Talk to you later."

Khori hadn't seen the type of glow his mother had with Kevin in a long time and he really enjoyed seeing her happy again. Just knowing she had someone was all that mattered to him and that he brought such a composed content to her spirit was a joy for him. Khori remembered as a kid Shalay went through her trials of bad relationships, with his father being completely non-existent his whole life, Ronnisha's father Levi couldn't stay away from the street life, Zachariah's sperm donor was a complete non-factor and his two little sister's dad only hung around when Shalay had liquor in the house. To see his mother not go for the flashy flare first and build a true relationship with a man that truly loves her for her was amazing not just for her but for Khori too. He respected Kevin like he was one of his uncles already and for him to be the man that makes his mother smile at the thought of him was all Khori needed.

Denise made it to her hotel suite with Ashley after leaving Sherell and Cedric at the hospital. Her little over excited daughter ran around in the hotel room, going through every room and opening every drawer or door to see what was in there. Denise relaxed in the living room area on the sofa, just trying to self-meditate while her daughter dart back and forth from one spot to the next. Right when everything started to quiet down for her the sound of a text notification went off on her phone. Thinking it was Yolanda or maybe Sherell checking on her, Denise reached for her phone in her purse.

"So, you in town with my child and you can't let me know? I want to see Ashley before you leave again", a text from Jamal.

Denise just looked at his text with disgust in her face, wondering how she could have fallen for such a man and wondering how did he know she was in town that fast. She didn't want to reply because Denise knew if she did it would go through a series of emotions for the both of them and she was too tired for the nonsense. She knew Jamal would start off sounding so sweet, asking how she's doing, can they work it out, telling her that he misses his girls and when he doesn't get the response, he thinks he should get then the anger surfaces. He starts blaming her for their break-up, accuses her of his nephew Garu's disappearance and threatens to take Ashley. Denise wasn't in the mood for the rollercoaster ride that was Jamal and understood why Sherell had nothing to do with him after Lamaj was born. She had to shake her head at herself, just thinking about how it is all connected between Sherell, Jamal and herself. Denise laughed and mumbled to herself,

"I couldn't make this shit up if I wanted to. I need to write a book."

She laid down on the sofa while her baby girl watched cartoons and thought about if she should allow Jamal to see Ashley before they go back to Houston in a week. Denise never wanted to be the baby mama that denies a man from seeing his child ever, even though she moved to Texas to avoid him altogether, she just didn't want the drama Jamal brings. She laid there contemplating the issue because she had a few days to decide but for now she was just going to enjoy being back home for a while and worry about that later.

Kevin was just leaving his parents' house with Renee when he heard the message Shalay left for him, he needed to hear her voice after the ordeal he just went through a while ago. His father was still adamant about Amanda not having any kind of custody over his grandchild, but Martin also told his son if the judge agrees with Amanda, they wouldn't have a choice. Ideas of paying someone off to beat and kidnap Amanda ran through Kevin's mind as he thought about the possibility of Amanda being able to take his daughter anytime she wanted to. Kevin needed to prove that Amanda was only going into this custody battle with him merely for visual benefit and not because she wanted to be a mother to a special needs child. He just didn't know what he had to do to convince the judge that allowing Amanda to have any kind of custody over Renee would be detrimental to the betterment of his daughter. It all was put to the back burner when Kevin seen the pure excitement in his daughter's eyes when they parked in front of Shalay's house. Renee barely gave Kevin time to put his car in park before she was removing her seat belt and opening the car door,

"Renee, I know you ready to see her but what I say?"

"Don't open the car door until it is off", replied an innocent face Renee.

Kevin gave her the signal that she could go, and Renee darted to the front door. Shalay opened the door and the two embraced like they haven't seen one another in years. After hearing that her makeshift little sisters were in the game room, Renee left to have fun while Shalay stood in the doorway looking at her man slowly walk up to her porch. Shalay thought Kevin was moving slow because he was drained from the events of the day, but he really was just admiring the complete love for his daughter he just witnessed. She put her soft gentle hands on the side of his face,

"Hey handsome, I missed you."

Kevin wrapped his woman in his arms, and they engaged in a passionate kiss. They were so enthralled into one another that the couple didn't see Khori walk up,

"Please get a room. Nobody wanna see all that."

Shalay laughed at her son and walked Kevin inside as they all got ready for the dinner Shalay cooked. More than anything, Kevin was just enjoying the fact that his daughter was able to enjoy a true family moment that didn't only involve her grandparents. Right before the family got all together, there was a knock at the door and after Zachariah answered it, he came back telling Kevin a woman was at the door for him. When Kevin got to the door animosity rushed through his body like a freight train as he stared down to the image of Amanda standing on the porch,

"Amanda, what are you doing here?"

"Well hello to you too Kevin. My personal detective told me you were here, and I just wanted to talk with you and commend you on how you kept your cool today. I was really trying to push your buttons and you didn't budge. I'm not stopping until I'm with my daughter again", replied Amanda.

Kevin couldn't believe how cocky his evil baby mama was being as she told him she had a personal one on one with the judge that was overseeing their case. She continued to tell him how it wasn't looking good for him to have total custody of Renee because the judge felt that a child should always have their mother in their lives. Kevin was done talking with Amanda,

"You need to leave, and we will settle all of this in court."

"Aww, you wanna get back to your colored girlfriend and her little monkeys. You always were one to run to them kind of people. I must have been the last piece of good white pussy you ever had huh", responded Amanda as she stepped off the porch.

Kevin was livid and it showed all over his face as he stood watching Amanda drive away. He stood on the porch attempting to gain his composure before stepping back into the house because he didn't like anyone seeing him so upset. Khori walked outside to check on Kevin,

"You good Kev?"

"I'm good lil bro. I just know I can't let this racist bitch be anywhere near my child", replied Kevin.

Khori was a little confused on the racist part because he never heard anyone say that Renee's mother was ever racist. When Kevin explained the whole episode of events that took place on the porch, Khori immediately went to his laptop in the house,

"Say Kev, technology is a motherfucka."

Khori explained to Kevin that after he and his mother reconnected, he installed a security system at her house. He told Kevin that the system had video as well as audio. Once Khori started pulling up the different camera angles, he began to rewind the video to the exact moment Amanda stepped onto the porch. They didn't see her but Shalay walked up behind Kevin when Khori pressed play on the screen and they all listened as Amanda spoke about the custody battle. It was a complete punch in the face for Shalay once she heard Amanda call her the "colored girlfriend" and that her kids were "little monkeys".

"This bitch bout to get all this work. Oh, bitch I want all the smoke", blurted out Shalay as she stormed off.

Khori hurried up and closed the laptop and Kevin went to console his woman. He caught up to Shalay as she paced in the living room, furious at the fact that this woman called her children animals. Kevin slowly went up to her and just held her in his arms as he repeatedly told her it will all be alright. He had finally got something against Amanda that would damage her image in court, and he could feel the weight just fall off. They stood there in the living room as Kevin suggested that they go enjoy dinner with their kids but Shalay had one last thing to say,

"Y'all might not make it to the court room. Cause if I see the bitch on the street, I'm fucking her up on sight. I'm a kick her fucking teeth in."

Kevin just smiled as he kissed his girl, gave her a love tap on the ass and they went in the dining room to enjoy dinner. Khori made several copies of the porch incident before joining everyone.

CHAPTER 10

It had been almost a week since Cedric's emergency room visit and he was more than happy to finally be cleared by his doctor to get back to normal activities. He and Devin both had doctor's appointments that day, so they made it a day for them to hang together. They had just finished with their doctors and were making their way through the lobby when Cedric seen an old high school classmate. Devin stood there in awe of how extremely well put together this woman was as Cedric gave her a hug,

"Leslie what you doing around here?"

"Hey Ced, just going have lunch with my sis. How have you been baby", replied Leslie.

"I've been good. Girl you look good as always."

Leslie and Cedric been knowing each other since high school, he was the main reason Leslie's sister was one of the head accountants in Cedric's department and Leslie always returned the favor by giving Kareem first dibs on any special packages she can find for him because she worked for a shipping and storage company. Cedric was standing in the lobby talking with Leslie and Devin couldn't take his eyes off of her. Leslie's deep brown cinnamon toned skin was flawless, the hazel-colored eyes simply sparkled, her lips could boldly carry the ominous nickname of "soup coolers" and her body shape could give an hourglass a run for its money. Devin was a young and strong 24-year-old man, but he had a weakness for an older woman that kept herself together. Devin didn't find women his age attractive because he felt they weren't on his level mentally and most of the time all they seen was the celebrity athlete not the man. The two talked for a brief moment but Leslie had to get to her sister and Cedric was heading out the door with Devin, so they gave each other a hug again as they said their goodbyes. Devin just smiled when Leslie walked away to the elevator and couldn't help but to ask,

"Now that right there is one sexy ass woman, who the hell was that Unk?"

"She's way out of your league nephew, trust me you not ready for her. Besides she's my age or maybe older, let's go fool", laughed Cedric as he headed for the exit doors.

They headed to Devin's truck, making plans to grab some lunch when Kevin called Cedric about Amanda. Cedric had heard about the incident on Shalay's porch and was just as fed up with Amanda's antics as Kevin was. Kevin told his friend that Renee's mother was still trying to pursue joint custody of his daughter even after Kevin's attorney showed the evidence to the judge. Cedric tried to ease his friend's stress by cracking jokes as he told him that he should just let Shalay beat Amanda up and chase her out of town. Kevin understood what his buddy was trying to do but at the moment the thought of Amanda poisoning his daughter's mind with her degrading mentality shadowed him. It pained Cedric to see the lively spirit Kevin usually carried be dwindled down to ash by one person's actions and the decision that could change his life could be made by a man that doesn't know him or his daughter.

Khori went to visit his lovely grandmother while everyone else in the family was at work or running errands of their own. He enjoyed just being with Delores by himself with no other distractions because she can focus on him and him alone, not that he wanted her all to himself but that it was less stressful on her. Khori walked with his grandma to the atrium with her arm locked in his as he just caressed her soft wisdom filled hand. Delores just went on and on about her husband, her children and how raising her kids alone was a challenge but a blessing at the same time. Khori listened while she went on about her childhood living in New Orleans and how it used to be. He always loved his grandmother's stories but this time it was different for him because it was like she was spilling out every memory she had. Delores' stories jumped from decade to decade and back again as she went on with her life experiences in a random order to Khori. He knew they didn't have much longer together and every visit meant more to him than it ever could mean to her, so he listened to ever word. The sounds of water from the small flowing creek in the atrium area was drowned out by the sweet sound of Delores' voice to Khori's ear but then the inevitable occurred and she couldn't remember who he was when she referred to him as being one of his uncle Kareem's classmate. Khori knew it was time for his visit to end and he gestured for the nurse he hired to come help him get his grandmother back to her room. After sitting Delores in her favorite rocking chair, Khori gave his grandma a loving kiss on the forehead and the nurse could see he was fighting back the tears. She attempted to make him feel better as they walked out of Delores' room,

"One thing I can say, this was the longest conversation she has held with someone in a while. You are truly special to her baby."

Khori thanked the nurse and made his way to his driver waiting outside for him. When he got in the tinted SUV outside the nursing home Semaj called him joking about the incident that happened with Kevin and Amanda. Semaj overheard his mother talking to his aunt about it and was laughing with Khori about how Shalay still wanted to fight Amanda over calling her kids "little monkeys". Talking and laughing with his cousin really helped Khori out of the funk he was stuck in,

"Dude I really needed that laugh."

"You and Devin still coming over later tonight for y'all artwork right", asked Semaj.

Khori remembered he had Semaj put together a piece he been wanting to get tatted for a while and his younger cousin came up with the perfect piece, so they agreed to meet up later that day before ending their call. Khori's driver was bringing him back to his hotel, where Erica was waiting for him, when the driver mentioned that he seen a man taking photos of Mr. Talport on the porch with the woman. Khori found it strange and brushed it off as they pulled up to the front of his hotel, the only thing running through his mind was getting to Erica. Walking into his hotel room to the sight of Erica relaxing on the sectional in the living room watching TV was all Khori needed to bring him to his complete Zen. He never realized until just now how Erica centers him to the point that any stress, affliction or trial simply falls to the waist side when he's around her. Erica looked up at her lover standing in front of her and without them saying one word to one another they communicated everything to each other. She just patted her hand on the cushion of the sofa, suggesting Khori to sit down and he nestled himself right next to her. Erica laid his head between her bosom while softly stroking his face and Khori's mother Shalay ringed in his head. Enjoying every bit of the attentive affection he was receiving Khori asked,

"You do know the way I feel about you, right?"

Erica just smiled and continued holding Khori in her arms while listening to him confess everything to her like he was pouring out his soul. He hadn't said the words yet, but Erica knew what he was saying to her and it meant a lot but then Khori mustered up,

"You've been there for me since day one and I couldn't have asked for a better partner in crime. You bring me down when I get to high on my horse and you bring me up when you find me too low. You know my sentences before I could finish them and as crazy as I act sometimes you know how to match my crazy when it's needed. I don't think I've ever told you, but I love you for all you do. I love you as my woman, I love you as my friend, I love you as my business partner and I love you for the person you are. Erica Pleasant would you do me the greatest honor and become more to me than just a partner but become my life companion? Baby I love you and I can't see myself without you in it."

Khori opened a ring box he had tucked in his pocket and revealed to the now shocked Erica an engagement ring that sparkled like a star as he kneeled in front of her. Erica's eyes filled with tears as Khori waited on her response, but words escaped her while she looked down at the ring resting in his hand. She held out her left hand and he placed it on her finger, the fit was absolutely perfect. Erica wrapped her arms around her fiancé,

"You are my everything and just to make it clear, my answer is yes, yes, yes."

After his nephew Devin dropped him off at home, Cedric was chilling and found himself bored looking at sport channels and infomercials. He texted his wife to check on her while she was at work, texted his little brother and then caught himself texting Denise. Even after all the things that happened between them, Cedric still held a place in his heart for his ex and the fact that she stopped everything to come see him when he was in the hospital made him truly appreciate her. Cedric didn't know about the situation with Denise's baby daddy harassing her and his text came in right on time as she was trying to avoid calls from Jamal. Their messages went back and forth about the kids, work and just life in general until Denise's next text came through like a bombshell,

"I just want to apologize. We truly had a good thing, and I took it all for granted."

Cedric's heart sunk as he read the words, then he read them again, but he didn't have a response for her. He paused with texting her because he partially took the blame for their failed marriage for the past 6 years and was content with her not ever apologizing for her actions. Cedric knew the long working hours, never being home when she needed him, not communicating with her often like he should and even the lack of sexual attention was part of the problem with their marriage. Their failed marriage helped him become a better husband for his current wife and Cedric found the right reply as he typed,

"We go through things to better us as people and our marriage was a needed trial for us to go through to better us both. We both now know what we want and what we need. I love you for that, no apology needed."

His words went through her like a hot knife would butter but not in a bad way because Denise understood what he meant and appreciated it. She asked him if it was possible that they see each other before she makes the flight back to Houston and as much as Cedric wanted to say yes, he politely turned down the invite. Denise knew it wouldn't have been a good idea for them two to be together anyways and found it to be for the best. They continued to text each other talking about little Ashley and Tre growing up so fast, about Cedric's mother and even laughing about them both trying to find her a man in Texas. Denise was torn up about losing a good man like Cedric and falling for a man like Jamal. Their little conversation made that so evident, but she was pleased that they were able to salvage a friendship from the broken relationship they had.

Semaj had set up an appointment with his brother and cousin to get their tattoos done but the true exciting part for him was introducing Diamond to his family. They've been just enjoying one another's company for now and neither ever really mentioned meeting any of the family yet. Semaj didn't want to make it out of a big deal so he didn't tell Diamond who the two men were that was coming over to the shop, but she had a feeling they had to be important for Semaj to close up his shop for just two people. She was helping him prep his equipment before his clients walked in and Diamond started a live broadcast on one of her social media sights promoting Artistic Creations INC, because of her large following the views started climbing. Semaj was comfortable with his girl's premium paid sights because it brought in a lot of money from guys that just like to watch or girls that just want to try out what new things Diamond has. He was so comfortable with it that sometimes Semaj has taken the "not safe for work" pics or videos Diamond uses because he understood it was the business she was in and he was content with that. Just like Diamond was comfortable with the occasional nipple or clitoris piercings Semaj had to perform in the shop. She felt if her man could be relaxed about her masturbating on a video while getting paid to do so, she could be unbothered about him being face to face with another woman's vagina while his fingers hold her clit. They seemed perfect for each other and the strong self-esteem they both carried seemed to strengthen their relationship. They were sitting in the back of the shop when Semaj heard a knock at the door and he went to answer it, Diamond instantly heard the laughter of her man and two other men. When the guys made it to the back of the shop where Semaj's studio area was Diamond seen one guy that was fairly good looking, well dressed and had a businessman attitude about him. The other guy was a juggernaut, muscles from head to toe, with a cast on his right arm and the only thing she was thinking at the time was,

"Who the hell broke the hulk's arm?"

She let out an innocent smile while Semaj introduced her to his brother Devin and his cousin Khori. The guys got themselves relaxed while greeting Diamond and she couldn't help but to ask as she looked at Semaj's brother,

"Devin? You look like you should be on somebody's front four defensive line, like for real."

The guys all laughed at her comment as Semaj replied,

"He is, he's one of Denver's best pass rushers ever."

Diamond was a little embarrassed that she didn't recognized the guy and apologized but Devin wasn't bothered by it one bit. Devin even cracked a joke that his cousin Khori was more popular than him and no one recognizes him at all. Khori looked over to his cousin as he laughed at Devin's remark,

"Semaj, can we go get our tatts now cause ya brother trying to clown me."

Diamond now was curious as to what Khori does after Devin's comment and asked him. When Khori told her that he's the founder and CEO of one of Denver's largest cannabis dispensaries she was floored to be in the same room with him. She had heard of a young guy named Kush from New Orleans that started his own company but never seen him before. To say that the two guys sitting in front of her were millionaires was astonishing because they were nothing like what she would have imagined a millionaire to be. No big flash or flair, no large entourage following them, just two regular mild-mannered guys enjoying life and family. Devin was first in the chair as Semaj started his machine up to tattoo his brother when Khori asked

Diamond what she does. She giggled thinking of a way to tell them,

"The p.c. version is called being an exotic entertainer, but I call it being a stripper. My true goal is opening up a dance studio, choreography for the kids and pole dancing for the adults."

"Well alright nah. My buddy Ricky is a bouncer at a club called The Rabbit Hole", replied Devin.

Diamond laughed as she told him that that's the exact place she dances at and that they should come for a special show tonight because her best friend is making a debut performance. They all sat back and enjoyed each other's company while Semaj went to work on the tattoos he designed for Devin and Khori. Diamond noticed they both were getting the same thing and asked what it was for but when Khori started talking about his little sister Ronnisha, Diamond could still see the pain in his eyes. She remembered the fatal incident because she was at the church fair when it happened, and it touched her because she was the same age at the time of the girl Khori was referring to. Diamond reached out to hold Khori's hand,

"Me and my mother attended her funeral, I'm so sorry for all of your loss."

"Alright cuz, this one is a keeper", smiled Khori.

Devin started to lighten the mood with stories of his little brother when they were young and all of them were embarrassing for Semaj. Diamond was enjoying every bit of the time spent with Semaj's brother and cousin but now she was anxious to see how he would interact with her family.

Kareem was heading over to pick up Cedric so that they all could hang out with Devin, Khori and Semaj. What he didn't tell his older brother, or his sister-in-law was that they were going to a strip club. Kareem knew Sherell had no problem with Cedric hanging out with the guys tonight but having half naked women all around him might have changed her mind. Cedric reluctantly joined his little brother for the outing because he knew Kareem had something up his sleeve but with Devin heading back to Denver in two days, Cedric had to go. Kareem was on the phone with Khori when Cedric got in the car,

"Yeah, the old man just got in."

"Who da hell you calling old sucka?"

"Who da hell says sucka anymore", laughed Khori.

They all laughed on the phone while Kareem made his way downtown and Cedric asked where they were going. His little brother just smiled and continued driving without saying a word but Khori made it very clear over the phone. When Cedric heard gentleman's club, a small evil grin appeared because he knew he was about to see some naked ass but when he heard they would be meeting his nephew's girlfriend also, confusion kind of set in. Cedric didn't know what to say but Khori had nothing but good things to say about the young lady he met at Semaj's tattoo studio. They all managed to pull up to The Rabbit Hole Gentleman's Club at the same time and Devin was already there standing out front talking with his old teammate Ricky. The bouncer waived all of their entrance fees and let the Daniels crew in the club. The club was jumping with excitement, beautiful ladies walking around, and the DJ kept everyone entertained. Semaj seen his lady waiting at the bar for him and he happily introduced her to his uncles. Diamond gave her usual cute smile as she said hi and ordered all the guys some drinks to start them off. Cedric hadn't been to a strip club since his bachelor party and Kareem joked around stating,

"This is where I want my bachelor party to be, I'm just saying."

The brothers enjoyed the scenery with their nephews as Diamond had one of the waitresses set up a table in front of the main stage for them. The club was laid out with all the exquisite elements in a semi-circle with leather recliners accompanied with square wrought iron side tables between every other chair. The main stage, that had chairs all around it, was elevated just enough that when the customers sat at it, they had to look up at the dancers on the hardwood floor stage that resembled a basketball court floor. The presence of Fleur-de-Lis and Mardi Gras masks decorated the entire club in different colors or styles as the essence of New Orleans could be felt in every corner of the building. Cedric and Kareem felt like VIP's being catered to with drinks and dancers coming over just to say hello. Diamond rushed over in excitement and sat in Semaj's lap as she whispered,

"She's about to perform."

A spotlight came on and focused directly to the back of the stage and the DJ came across the speaker system,

"This ya boy DJ Felt-Tip and we have a special performance for you tonight here at The Rabbit Hole. Coming to you for the first time ever on any stage I'd like to introduce you to this chocolate diva and exotic flower, Lotus!"

The curtains parted with the artist Lotus standing there for all the audience to see the exquisite specimen of a woman shining in the spotlight's glow. Her freshly manicured dreds draped over her chocolate shoulders, as the vibrant yellow and red two-piece bikini contoured her thick immaculate figure that demanded the eyes of everyone. The Daniels' boys have seen their share of sexy, fine and sensual women before, but this performer Lotus was all of that plus more, she was the definition of alluring. The music began to play thru the sound system, and it caught Cedric off guard because of the old school sound,

"Say man, she is not about to dance to Silk Lose Control, what she know about that?"

Diamond leaned over by Cedric and told him that most of Lotus' music selection is 90's R&B or Hip Hop,

"She said she really feels that style of music, old soul I guess."

As the music played on everyone's attention was glued to the stage, as Lotus performed. Once Kareem took his eyes off the extremely sexy body, he looked at her face and realized it was the pretty delivery girl with the razors that came to his shop a while ago,

"I know her."

The dancer smiled and stared in Kareem's eyes as she looked like she was dancing just for him. She got down on all fours and crawled to the edge of the stage, gesturing for Kareem to come to her. Resisting her command seemed ridiculous as he walked up to her and she wrapped her legs around his waist, pulling him closer. As the exotic dancer slow grinded to the music, staring Kareem deep into his eyes, Lotus pulled loose the string that held her top on, revealing two succulent chocolate 38C sized breast that screamed for attention and then she laid back onto the stage caressing her body in front of him. Kareem reached into his pocket and pulled out a small wad of cash, sprinkling it all over the dancer's sensual body, Devin joined him with throwing an open band of ones in the air on stage also. Diamond was beyond ecstatic for her friend's first time on stage and shouted her name so that everyone knew who she was,

"Let's get it Lotus!"

But Lotus' performance wasn't done just yet when the DJ changed the tempo with an upbeat hip hop song. An old school Uncle Luke song blared through the speakers and the crowd went into an uproar as the dancer blessed the stage with a thunderous split that transitioned into some strong New Orleans' "p-popping" but everybody else calls it twerking. Cedric caught himself singing along,

"Face down ass up, that's the way we like to fuck!"

The performer continued to do tricks, stunts and splits until the song ended with Diamond giving her friend a standing ovation, right along with everyone else in the club. Devin was thoroughly impressed with the dancer Lotus' coming out performance that he walked up to the stage while she was collecting all of her money off the floor and placed two stacks of ten-dollar bills at her feet. Khori couldn't be out done by his cousin so he pulled out three stacks of ten-dollar bills and handed it to the new exotic dancer as he smiled,

"Baby girl, you are a beast on that stage. I couldn't take my eyes off of you."

The dancer blushed as she thanked him and Diamond came running up hugging her friend, congratulating her on a great performance. Devin seen a whole new side of the experience of a dance performance and went to his little brother,

"Lil bro, this is what your girl does? I gotta say, I'm impressed and ole girl on stage fine as hell."

"Diamond actually taught her everything", replied Semaj.

The group stayed a little longer to enjoy some drinks while Diamond entertained them by getting a few dancers to give the guy's lap dances, it turned out to be a very interesting night.

Everybody was leaving the club after Diamond's friend Lotus performance when Denise called Cedric's cell. She came over as sounding extremely nervous and Cedric could hear banging in the background. Denise told him that Ashley's father was at the door demanding to see his daughter and that he was drunk. Cedric wanted to get involved but Kareem advised him not to because of Cedric and Jamal's previous encounters. Devin agreed with his uncle's decision that Cedric stay out of it because of his health and volunteered to go over to check on Denise. He joked with Cedric stating,

"Unk you don't need to be over by Denise at this time of night anyways. Sherell find out you was over there, and it's gone be some smoke in the city."

"Dude prolly be gone by the time you get there, or his ass gone burn off once he see yo big ass", laughed Kareem.

Devin chuckled as he got in his truck and Cedric gave him the address to the hotel Denise was staying. He told his uncles he'll let them know that everything is okay once he gets there as he pulled off and Cedric let Denise know Devin's on his way. Still reminiscing over the images of the dancer Lotus he seen just moments ago, Devin tried to focus on getting to Denise's hotel room to make sure she's safe from her baby daddy. But the chocolate exotic dancer lingered in the back of his mind and he texted Semaj,

"Say lil bro, give ole girl my number. I'm trying to shoot my shot with her for real."

Semaj sent back a laughing emoji as a response to his brother's text and Devin continued to his destination as he pulled in the parking lot of the hotel. He made his way down the hallway to Denise's room after stepping off the elevator expecting to hear some sort of disturbance. Devin walked down the walkway looking to see Jamal standing by the door, but no one was there when he knocked. He could hear shuffling behind the door right before Denise partially opened it with the security latch still engaged. Devin smiled at her and Denise unlocked the door as she let him in,

"Thank you so much for coming over. I guess someone in another room called the front desk cause hotel security told him he had to leave but I just have a feeling that clown gone show back up."

"It's cool, I'm a sit over here with you for a while just to make sure everything stays quiet", replied Devin as he texted his uncles that everything was clear.

Little Ashley could hear her mother talking to someone in the front of the hotel room as she slipped out of the bedroom and sat on the sofa. Devin and Denise walked in the living room from the kitchenette area to Ashley curled up on the sofa looking at TV. Devin sat on one side of Ashley and Denise on the other side when she told her daughter that she needs to go to bed because they will be leaving to go back home in the morning. Ashley laid her head on Devin's shoulder, rubbed her little fingers against the cast on his arm as she innocently asked,

"You hurt yourself?"

"I had an accident at work", replied Devin as he put his arm around Ashley, and she fell asleep on him.

Denise admired how Devin just took to Ashley so quick and watched as he rocked her into a deep sleep. Once Devin realized that Denise's baby girl was sound to sleep, he picked her up, laid her in the soft bed and closed the door behind him, as he made his way to the exit door. Denise was sitting on the sofa with her face buried in her hands when Devin walked back in the living room. He thought she was just sleepy until she looked up at him and Devin seen it was far from Denise being tired. Her eyes were bloodshot red with tears making their way down her face creating a river of sadness. Right then Devin understood his good deed wasn't quite done as he sat next to Denise and wrapped his arms around her. Denise did like her daughter did moments ago and laid her head on Devin's chest as she cried,

"The devil is real because the guy that was beating at my door and calling me all types of names had to be the devil. I just know that wasn't the man I was infatuated with 6 years ago."

Devin just made himself comfortable, held Denise in his arms and listened as Denise poured out her soul to him. She told him how sweet Jamal use to be with her and how he changed, even told Devin about the Garu situation. They talked until they both drifted off to sleep on the sofa and Devin woke to Denise nestled on top of him. She had made herself completely comfortable, with her head resting in his chest, her arms wrapped around him and her legs draped over his. He didn't notice before because he was strictly concerned with Denise's safety and well-being but now that it's all calm, Devin seen how sexy Denise was at the moment. She was laying on him with some knee-high cartoon socks on, silk white boy shorts that just covered her plump round ass and a loose fit wife – beater that revealed some smooth sensual side boobs, but her nipples were poking at the shirt. Devin hand slid down her back, softly caressing her skin, until it reached her lower back right above her ass. He moved her soft curly hair from her face as she slept, Denise was absolutely beautiful to him. Devin just laid there staring at her, wanting to do nothing more than taste her soft lips but then he pulled himself back,

"Nigga, what the fuck are you doing? This is yo uncle ex-wife fool."

He started to pull himself out of the trance she had put him in but then she opened them big pretty brown eyes and he was pulled right back in. In the process of Devin rubbing on Denise's back, his manhood stiffened so hard to the point that it was pressing against her as she was laying right on top of it. His gentle caresses felt so good to her at the moment because it's been over a year since Denise has been in a strong man's arms. Devin was definitely the definition of a strong man as Denise's hands rubbed up his chest and his masculinity no longer had him looking like a little boy to her. She crawled her way up the mountain of a man until they were eye to eye and she ever so softly kissed his lips. Their lips locked, their tongues began to explore one another, the passion was so intense that the room felt warmer but then Denise fully woke realizing what was happening and stopped herself. She sat up,

"Oh my God! What the hell am I doing? We can't do this, we can't."

Still straddled on him, Denise could feel nothing but massive dick pressing on her juice box and the battle was lost, flesh won. Devin held onto her ass and the kissing started up again while Denise's hips slowly rotated. Fed up with the schoolgirl dry humping, Devin sat up on the sofa and pulled Denise's top over her head revealing two succulent upright caramel toned breast. She pressed his face in her homegrown pleasure pillows and Devin immediately found her nipple as his tongue circled around, sending chills down her spine. The passion level increased to aggression when Denise tore Devin's button-down shirt open and all the years of weightlifting stared her in the face. Devin was a chiseled specimen of a man and every muscle could be individually identified as Denise's hands slid over his mocha toned skin. They both knew they had gone too far but the ecstasy they were feeling was too much to deny themselves. Denise reached down to unbuckle Devin's jeans and her eyes widened when her fingers wrapped around a thick tube steak resting between his legs. She pulled it from his boxers, as it laid on his stomach and all in one motion, she held it upright as he moved her shorts to the side while she slid down on the enlarged vein. He was in deeper than she had ever felt, and it showed on her face when they made eye contact. She took her time sliding up and down as the curve of his dick moved between her juicy walls, filling her up. Devin was three minutes in a glorious position and knew if Denise kept grinding her hips their escapades would be over sooner than later. He laid her on the sofa, slid her shorts off and a delicious sight stared him down. It felt like he snatched her soul from her when Devin latched onto her clit, the only thing Denise could say was,

"You got to be fucking kidding me."

Devin's whirlwind of tongue tricks forced Denise to reach down and hold on as the orgasmic ride took her to the brink of screaming in pleasure. She had to stay quiet, so with one hand Devin reached up to cover her mouth while he devoured her pussy and Denise came in a spastic fashion, shivering on his lips. Devin then continued with the pleasure, as he turned her over and slid his meat back in, slowly filling her up with every inch he had as he hit it from the back. The combination of rock-solid muscle and supple moist flesh mixed between them until Devin pulled out, exploding all over Denise's ass. They both collapsed from exhaustion with elated smiles painted on their faces but then the reality of what just happened came full circle as the taboo couple realized what they've just done. The eerie silence as the two began to get dressed was evident that they had their regrets but when Devin stood at the door to leave all Denise seen was a sexy mountain of a man that brought her to an all-new level of erotica. She placed her hand on his chest as he leaned in to kiss her,

"Will I be seeing you in Houston or is this the last time?"

"I never had any reason to visit Houston before but now I believe I do", replied Devin.

CHAPTER 11

Khori invited his mother to have lunch with him and Erica because he wanted to tell her face to face about their engagement. Shalay and Kevin were finishing up some paperwork with some new business clients when Khori called but they were happy to join him for lunch. Erica was excited to share with Shalay that she and Khori was planning to get married because she didn't have a mother to share it with herself. She really connected with Khori's mother the last time they had a sit down and to share this with her was thrilling for Erica. Khori was just ready to run to the courthouse and get it over with but he knew once he tell his mother, she was gonna go all out for her firstborn wedding. The young couple waited at the bar & grill patio restaurant for their lunch companions to arrive when Khori seen Kevin parking his car. Shalay stepped out, looking as wonderful as always and seen her handsome son waiting for her,

"I hope you ready to spend cause I'm hungry hungry."

Khori laughed and walked his mother to where they were sitting as Erica stood to greet everyone coming to the table. A waitress came over to get everyone's drink order before taking down food request and Shalay could tell something was up because Erica couldn't get rid of the big smile she had stuck to her face. Khori started the conversation off by thanking his mother and Kevin for joining them as he nervously spoke to them. Shalay's beau smiled as he could see the young guy was fidgety,

"Wha cha got going on youngin'?"

Before Khori could get out one more word, Shalay seen the skating rink sized engagement ring on Erica's left ring finger and screamed in joy. She grabbed hold of her future daughter-in-law's hand with tears in her eyes and delight all over her face. Erica was so happy to see the excitement on Shalay's face as she began to run down wedding ideas, venues, pastors and the perfect time. The two couples were enjoying their time together at the restaurant but then a dark cloud came to their table in the image of Amanda LeBlanc. She carried an evil smile as she stood in front of them,

"Now look what we have here. Isn't this just the cutest thing. Kevin you never cease to amaze me with your charitable acts. Sitting here showing the common folk a better life."

"Bitch, I done had enough of yo shit", replied Shalay.

Amanda laughed as she told Kevin to control his little pet. At that moment Kevin and Shalay stood up to address Amanda physically but Khori rushed to step in front of them both,

"Ms. LeBlanc you really haven't learned your lesson yet, have you? You came to my mother's house trying to provoke Mr. Talport and we showed the judge your vulgar acts. Now you just pop-up at the exact place we're having lunch and again you try to provoke him. This is really starting to look like harassment ma'am."

"Little boy you do not know who I am or what I can get done, do you."

Khori briefly smiled as he stared into Amanda's eyes,

"Evidently ma'am you do not know who I am, let me give you a clue. I'm the guy that had you recorded for the first incident you ran your mouth, the same guy that secretly informed your private investigator that Kevin would be at this very restaurant today and the very same guy that has a security driver recording you along with your photographer right now. See I deal with your type a lot in my multimillion-dollar business, the entitled. Always feel they're better and smarter than everybody else but in actuality y'all the lowest of the low. See you thought if you could provoke Mr. Talport into looking violent on camera then the judge might sway in your favor of giving you precious Renee completely but see the tables have turned my dear and you're looking very aggressive in our eyes. So aggressive that a child isn't safe around you. So, before I say fuck it and let my beautiful mother beat yo ass like she so wants to right now, I recommend you leave and never darken our area again. Oh, and rest assure that the judge will have colored photos of this event. You do like that word, colored?"

Amanda stormed away walking back to the car and noticed Khori's security driver confiscating the camera from her private investigator. She seen that she was outsmarted by Kevin's companions and knew their day in court tomorrow was going to be a rough one. Khori sat back down at the table with his family and enjoyed the rest of their time there. Shalay was completely overjoyed at how her son handled the situation and Kevin was thankful beyond measures towards Khori.

Kareem was waiting for his nephew Devin to come through before his flight back to Colorado in a few hours. Devin had already made his rounds to seeing everyone and saying goodbye, but he saved his uncle Kareem last because Kareem wanted to give him a haircut before he leaves. Yolanda and Kareem were chilling at the shop because Yolanda was also waiting on her sister to stop by before taking her flight back to Houston. The forbidden couple hadn't spoken to each other since the electrifying night and didn't know they were both heading to the same spot. Denise arrived first and little Ashley darted straight through the shop to her uncle Kareem to give him a big hug. Yolanda was in the back office organizing Kareem's chaotic desk when Denise walked in,

"Girl do you ever stop working?"

"Not with this man of mine and all his rubbish", replied Yolanda as she hugged her sister.

They sat down in the office just having small talk and discussing how ignorant Jamal been the few days she's been back. Devin walked in the salon and Kareem patted his hand in the barber chair he was next to. He jumped in the chair as Kareem covered him in the barber cape and started touching up Devin's hair. Kareem mentioned to Devin that Denise just came over to say goodbye also and was in the office with Yolanda. The young bull almost had his uncle mess up his hair when he quickly turned his head to get a glimpse of Denise behind him,

"Whoa boy! Almost took out a plug of ya hair."

Ashley ran up when she seen Devin sitting in the chair and asked to see his cast again but this time when he showed her the little Princess pulled out a pink marker. She drew a flower with a heart and her name on his cast,

"See, now it's pretty."

Devin thanked the little angel for her artwork while Kareem finished up on his haircut.

"C'mon Ash, it's time to go baby", stated Denise as she walked out from the back.

The two secret lovers locked eyes and anyone with a bit of common sense could see the sexual tension between them. Denise's heart fluttered at the sight of Devin and his entire body tingle as she walked by.

"Hey Devin, it was nice seeing you and thank you so much for last night. I really needed our talk."

"Anytime", replied Devin.

Yolanda suspiciously looked at her sister because something just didn't seem right and walked her out to her car. She knew Devin went over to her hotel because Kareem told her after he got back from the club with Cedric, but the way Denise mentioned "their talk" was a little suspect. After getting Ashley in the car, Yolanda gave her sister a look and asked her what happened when Devin got to her room. Denise ran down the event but as soon as she mentioned Devin putting Ashley to sleep and they started talking about Jamal she started stuttering over her words.

"Denise, tell me you didn't fuck this boy."

Yolanda's little sister's eyes bucked at the statement and Yolanda put her head down,

"Denise, Denise, Denise out of all the men in the Greater New Orleans area you had to fuck your ex-husband's nephew? Really? You couldn't find any other dick?"

Denise was stuck trying to explain herself and didn't have not one reply but when Yolanda asked was it at least worth it her response was,

"Yes! That freaking stallion blew my back out. That boy got inches I tell, fucking inches of meat and he put in work."

"I don't wanna hear no more, oh my God. Girl you nasty. Y'all please keep this between y'all", replied Yolanda.

The sisters hugged, said their goodbyes and Denise drove off to the airport with little Ashley in tow. Yolanda walked back in the shop, looked at Devin with a sinister smile and he knew right then that she knew about the night he had with her sister, but he also noticed she kept the information to herself.

Cedric and Sherell went to visit his mother at the nursing home, Lamaj was home from college to visit so he decided to stay home with his little brother. Sherell was concerned that Cedric would stress himself out if the visit with Delores didn't go well and her husband promised if he feels any kind of anxiety, he will cut the visitation short. When they arrived, they found the senior facility was in a very festive type of atmosphere with Mardi Gras Indians prancing around, a small second line band and even a few staff members in costume. The couple was a little baffled with the event because Mardi Gras was months away and asked the nurse what was going on. The cheerful nurse told them that Dr. Jackson likes to occasionally have festivities for his patients just to bring some fun into the facility. The blaring sounds of the horns from the band could be heard from every corner of the building and the bright colors of the Indian costumes brightened up every hallway. There was doctors and nurses just dancing along with patients through the halls and the smiles on their faces screamed joy. Cedric had never seen such a sight in a medical facility before and it was very pleasant to see as he made his way to his mother's room. When they arrived, they found Delores had pulled her rocking chair out and was sitting in the front of her room watching the makeshift parade go by. The look on her face was a delight to see, Cedric hadn't seen his mother so happy in a while and it brought everything into perspective, that family was the glue that held him together. She seen them walking up and happily waved them over as she began to get up out of her chair,

"Hey my babies."

Delores hugged and kissed them both as they watched the parade goers pass them by. Cedric's mother started to tell him about his father and being a part of the Zulu Social Club,

"Your father would have loved this right here. He always made sure to be part of every event, every ball and every second line. Anything that had to do with parade season he was all in."

Cedric just held onto his mother like a little kid would walking through a large crowd, loving every moment with her. Sherell asked Delores if she got involved in any of the festivals Cedric's dad was in when he was alive. The senior citizen told her she was the Zulu Club's head of treasury until she retired from the position after her husband's death. Delores said she couldn't be in a building that had almost as many memories in it with them together than their own home. She sat down back in her rocking chair to share some of the memories of Cedric's father to them as the last few Mardi Gras Indians and costumed goers passed them. Sherell had never had the chance to meet Cedric's father and every story about him was so intriguing to her because he sounded like a very caring man like her husband was. They sat and talked for what felt like hours, Sherell tidied up Delores' room while Cedric made tea for everybody and Delores continued on with her vivid stories. Cedric's loving wife would occasionally whisper in his ear to ask him if he was feeling okay and he would just nod his head yes with a smile. He never imagined letting his mother know he had a mild heart attack, and he was going to keep it that way. Cedric wanted to enjoy every pleasant moment he could have with his mother and telling her his medical issues was not part of the plan. They all laughed at stories Delores would talk about when Cedric was a little kid and Cedric would laugh about the whippings he would catch because of the crazy things he would do. Delores was enjoying her visitors, but the Daniels elder leaned in and whispered in her son's ear,

"Now baby you know I love me some Sherell, she is like a daughter to me. But where is Denise? You know that girl would have a hissy fit if she knew you was running the streets with Sherell. I know that's your friend, but you know how Denise gets baby."

"We okay mama, Denise at work right now and she told Sherell to come in her place", replied a smiling Cedric.

He knew it was time to call it a day and let his mother get some rest. On their way out the nurse was coming in to bring Delores her afternoon medicine and Cedric kissed his mother goodbye as he told her he'll be back another day. He felt good walking back to his car and Sherell could see a calm in her husband she hadn't seen in a while in him.

Semaj was in his studio and it was packed with clients, more than usual and he had no idea why. Everybody was looking to get a "Spice original" after they seen a video Diamond posted congratulating her bestie on her debut performance. In the video Lotus showed off her tattoo she received from Spice and the appointments started rolling in for him. He was just finishing a simple name tatt when his brother Devin called him before he got on his flight back to Denver. Semaj had seen his big brother that morning before he left and figured he was asking if he gave Lotus his number,

"Say big bro, I gave her your number, but ole girl just got out of a really bad relationship and she's really not looking for one right now."

"Nah bro, I didn't call for that. I need to chop it up with you real quick", replied Devin.

Semaj's sibling was concerned with Diamond's intent after hearing that she wants to open a dance studio for herself. He didn't want his little brother to become a victim of a con artist, thinking he's in love with someone that's really just out to use him for his money. Devin explained that he had seen men lose everything to parasites that drained them dry and that he was only trying to protect his little brother from an opportunist. Semaj took offense to the remarks because he knew Diamond was nothing how Devin had her portrayed. They talked about Diamond opening a dance studio and Semaj even offered to help her with start-up funds like his brother did for him, but Diamond refused the offer, wanting to do it solely herself. What Devin didn't know was that Diamond came from a single parent home, in which she watched as a young child, her mom does whatever it took to give them everything they needed. One principle she definitely took from her mother was,

"If you can't get it on your own, you don't need it",

 and Diamond kept that mentality all the time. Everything Diamond has, she bought with her own ends and prides herself on the fact that she never had to degrade herself or sleep with a man to get it. Being seen as an exotic dancer, most guys had the misconception that she was easy, and they couldn't have been any more wrong about her. She created herself like a person would a corporation, she saw a need and she supplied it, using every form of distribution to capitalize on. Diamond made money off of dancing on stage, paid social media sites, paid websites and even the occasional cameo in local music videos to get exactly what she needed. Semaj knew this and for his brother to come at him like he was weak or gullible was the part that pissed him off,

"Say big bro, trust me she doesn't need or want my little chump change. Shid, sometimes she offers to pay my bills when I talk about them and I have to tell her no. So, to make accusations that she's trying to get money out of me is totally out of line. She was just sharing with you her dreams and aspirations like she does with anyone she feels close to. I guess you just couldn't see pass her occupation to really see her. It's cool though, I understand everybody can't but me and her are good."

Devin felt bad after hearing his little brother side and apologized for doubting Semaj and Diamond's relationship before ending his call to get on his flight,

"Love you lil bro."

"Love you too big bro."

Cedric was heading over to Alonna's house for Sunday dinner with his family, everybody was meeting up there. It became a weekly tradition for one of the Daniels' kids to cook dinner for the whole family since their mother was in a nursing home and she couldn't do it anymore. Cedric was almost to his sister's house when Sherell made the comment about his nephew having a new girlfriend,

"Alonna found out Semaj dating a stripper. I wonder if he's gonna bring her to dinner tonight?"

"Huh?"

"You and Kareem didn't meet her last night?"

Cedric stayed quiet on the subject because he didn't want to discuss it in front of his always talkative little one sitting in the backseat. Sherell started talking about how she didn't really see anything wrong with the young lady's profession because she felt that strippers were very talented. Cedric gave his clueless wife a "please shut the hell up" look when their little man asked,

"Daddy what's a stripper?"

"Awe son, that's just somebody that takes the old paint off the wall before you put the new paint on", replied Cedric.

Sherell held her hand over her mouth as she laughed to herself while they parked in front of Alonna's house and Steven met them outside as everyone started getting out of the car. He gave little Tre a hug and right before darting in the house the energetic 5-year-old told his uncle,

"I wanna be a stripper when I grow up, mama say they real talented."

Cedric just put his head down as Sherell and Steven died laughing at the little boy's comment. Everyone started filing in one at a time as Alonna and Steven prepared a large soul food filled Sunday meal but the buzz in the adults' conversation was all about Semaj's new girlfriend. Alonna believed in allowing her kids to explore and learn from their own journeys but she didn't know how to feel about her son in a relationship with an exotic dancer. Kareem and Cedric tried to stay hushed on the issue because they didn't want their significant others to know they met the young lady already. Shalay was in the same mindset as her twin and had no problem expressing herself,

"I can't see taking my clothes off for money for some dirty old man to rub on me and what if my kids find out, what if my parents find out, what do I say? People gotta think about that."

"Mama your son made a business out of selling weed. I was very comfortable letting you know that's my job and when or if I have kids, they gone be comfortable too", replied Khori.

"But selling Marijuana how you do is a legal business."

"And so is being a stripper mama."

Khori caught his mother at a loss for words after his remark and then followed up by praising the young lady he met just a few nights ago. He told everyone how she's working on her second degree in Computer Science, that she wants to open up her own dance studio one day and how he sees potential in her to do it. Erica was curious as to when her fiancé met Semaj's girl and when he replied that he met her the night he hooked up with his uncles at the strip club The Rabbit Hole before Devin's flight all eyes were on the Daniels brothers. Kareem could feel Yolanda's eyes piercing the side of his face as he avoided eye contact and Cedric went into explanation mode as soon as Sherell heard what Khori said.

CHAPTER 12

Semaj had just picked Diamond up from her apartment and anxiety was advertised all over his face, as he made his way to his mother's house. He never imagined introducing his girlfriend to his family would be this hard, mainly because of the conversation he had with Devin and now Semaj is thinking everyone else would feel the same way about her. Semaj never mentioned to his girl what his brother said and wanted to keep it that way because he didn't want any ill feelings between the two. Diamond on the other hand was a little excited that Semaj was comfortable enough that he wanted her to meet the rest of his family, she even went so far as to bring thoughtful gifts for his mother and stepdad. The couple made their way through the Lower 9th ward, as Semaj drove pass his old elementary school, telling Diamond stories of his childhood and school crushes. But the attentiveness in Diamond could see her man was nervous and she just held onto his hand as they pulled up to his mother's house. Before he turned the car off Semaj looked her in the eyes,

"I'm telling you; we really don't have to go in there, my family is nuts and my aunt has no filters."

"Are you ashamed of me or what they may ask?"

"Of course, not baby, never that."

"Because you haven't met my mother yet and she is the spokesperson for no filters", replied Diamond.

They got out of the car with Diamond proudly holding her gift bags and Semaj noticed everybody was at his mother's house. He took a big sigh as he opened the door and walked into everyone gathering together in the kitchen as the younger kids had a run of the house. Alonna walked up to her son and gave him a kiss on the cheek as he introduced Diamond to her,

"Hey mama, this is Diamond."

The young lady standing in front of them was nothing like what they imagined, thinking she would show up half dressed in revealing body parts poking out but instead Semaj's girlfriend was dressed in a nice lady like casual dress, flats and calm soft make-up. Diamond could feel all the eyes on her in the house as she seen some familiar faces and gave them all the prettiest smile as Semaj introduced her to everyone. As Semaj presented her to his aunt Shalay the unfiltered twin came out as she asked Diamond if that was her real name or her stage name. Diamond laughed as she replied,

"My mama always said I was her precious gem when I was born, so she gave me a stripper name."

"I wanna be a stripper when I grow up, my mama said strippers are talented", replied the innocent little Tre as he walked pass Diamond.

The entire household fell out laughing as they heard Cedric's son say what he said. The ice was broken, and Diamond took the opportunity to give out the gifts she brought with her for Semaj's parents. From conversations with Semaj, Diamond knew Steven was a connoisseur of whiskey, so she gave him a bottle of limited-edition Johnnie Walker Blue Label and graced Alonna with a crystal necklace she got from a well-known spiritual wellness store Alonna frequently visits. Semaj's parents were so appreciative of the gifts and Khori walked up to his cousin,

"I told you, this one is a keeper."

The family all gathered together as everyone started getting their plates and Alonna happily dished the newcomer to the family her helping of everything cooked for Sunday's dinner.

After dinner was over, the guys found themselves all relaxing in the den sipping on their choice of adult beverage while all the women chilled on the patio outside sharing some bottles of wine. Diamond had found herself in the fold of the Daniels' clan as they talked about everything under the sun. Sherell shared her memories with the young newcomer right along with Yolanda sharing her experiences. Hearing it all out loud made it extremely funny or maybe it was just the wine talking as stories of the friendly co-worker becoming the new wife, the ex-wife's sister falling in love with the baby brother and then Shalay adding the cherry on top with the love affair with the best friend. Diamond started laughing hard to herself as she could hear her boyfriend's voice in her head saying his family is crazy. Shalay asked Diamond if she lived in New Orleans all her life and the young lady's reply shocked both of the twins.

"I grew up in the 7th ward, my full name is Diamond Sweed."

"7th ward? Ya mama name wouldn't be Darlene Sweed would it", asked Shalay.

Diamond was puzzled that Shalay knew her mother's name but quickly found out that the Daniels twin knew Diamond's mother very well. The young lady was completely thrown for a loop when Shalay told her that her daughter that died a few years ago was actually Diamond's cousin and the daughter of her uncle Ronald Levi Sweed. Diamond told them that her mother Darlene hadn't talk to her brother in almost two decades and she didn't know where or how to find him because her mother refused to help. Shalay figured Levi's lifestyle was partially the reason Diamond's mother parted ways with her own brother because it was the reason, she kept her daughter away from her father. The ladies made their way back inside to join the guys in the den, right when Kevin was making it known he had to leave and Shalay walked him outside. She knew her man had a very important day coming up and his nerves were getting to him,

"Baby everything is gonna work out just fine. Renee is your baby, shit she's our baby and anyone with eyes can see you've been there with her through it all. Nobody in their right mind would give that woman any kind of custody over her."

Shalay told him she will see him at the courtroom in the morning, Kevin kissed his lady before heading to his car and feeling so much better about the day to come. After watching Kevin pull off, Shalay went back inside to her family.

Delores woke from a sound sleep in a bed that wasn't hers and confusion set in instantly when she looked around the room to see nothing she recognized. The home she lived in for the past 30 plus years was nowhere to be found and Delores frantically searched for it as she got out of bed. The elderly woman stepped out of the bedroom into the living room area to see a young woman sitting on the couch dressed in purple scrubs. The nurse seen her patient shuffle through the room looking around puzzled and knew something was wrong,

"Hey Mrs. Daniels, everything okay?"

Delores didn't answer as she reached out for the knob of the front door and the nurse immediately responded by curbing her to sit down at the kitchen table with her. She could see the senior was uneasy about being in her strange surroundings as her eyes darted back and forth in the apartment, as if she was seeing everything for the first time. Just looking in her face, anyone could tell Delores was unfamiliar with everything around her and the medical assistant knew if she didn't try to get the patient centered, she was going to have a long night. The nurse attempted to retrieve some family photos Delores had in a photo album of her kids but as soon as the young woman wasn't in eyesight of her Delores bolted out the door into the hallway. Her patient was spiraling out of control and trying to get Delores to focus on a photo was out of the question. The nurse tried to just follow behind the wandering senior not to stop her but to only monitor her actions and keep Delores from harming herself. She walked pass a nurse's station, where an orderly seen the grandmother breeze across the counter he was sitting at. When he went to stop the elderly woman, the nurse close by gestured for him not to and Delores strayed on her way through the halls. Mumbling unrecognizable words as she marched on, Delores made her way to an empty dining hall and looked around as she sat at the first table she got to. The nurse sat down with her and told the orderly that was following close behind them both to go fetch them both some tea,

"Mrs. Delores loves the chamomile and hibiscus with honey. Can you please get us two cups?"

The caring nurse sat there holding and caressing Delores' hand while she looked around the dining area. Delores noticed the flowers resting as a centerpiece in the middle of the table and started talking about flowers her husband used to bring her. The nurse listened as Delores told stories of her husband when they were just dating and how he would do simple things that brought her so much joy. Delores' frantic state seemed to calm down as memories of the love she had for her husband flowed from her lips and the young nurse could see the light that was missing in her eyes return. They sat in the dining hall sipping their tea, talking about whatever topic tickled Delores' fancy and later they took their conversation back to her apartment where the grandmother talked herself to sleep.

After a lovely evening with his second family Kevin made his way to his parents' home to find an unwanted sight walking from the house. Amanda and her fiancé Alex were getting in their car as the headlights of Kevin's car beamed on them while he pulled into the curved driveway. Kevin didn't even bother turning the engine off as he sprung from the vehicle to address the couple, in an angered fashion but was met by his father before Kevin could get a word out. Kevin's nerves were on edge as his father Martin looked in his eyes and spoke,

"Son, you won. You won. She is pulling out and is only asking for visitation. We could put stipulations on that and make it supervised. You won, son."

A weight fell off Kevin's shoulders like a boulder as his body released the agony of the upcoming custody battle. He looked over to a tearful Amanda sitting in the car and Alex still standing outside as Kevin turned his car off. Alex walked up to Kevin with his hand extended out to shake his hand,

"Kevin first off, I just want to apologize for the whole ordeal. This could have all been avoided if we would have just sat down like adults and talked. Amanda truly feels bad about the whole thing and all she really wanted was to reconnect with her daughter, but she knows that's gonna take some time."

Kevin didn't know what to say after hearing Alex apologize for him and Amanda's actions as he went inside to see his daughter Renee and Alex walked back to his car to leave. Understanding the passion Kevin held was completely understood by Alex because he had a little sister with special needs himself and protecting her had become his primary goal. He created his foundation in Las Vegas strictly because of her and brought the concept of the foundation to New Orleans with him after funding a big business opportunity with the new casino boat that was built. Amanda told Alex about her daughter after they started dating and she explained to him how she was overwhelmed with the idea of raising a special needs child.

The thought of just leaving their child behind to some people is an unheard-of act but Alex understood that everyone isn't built for the challenge and the best thing for them is to just walk away. He seen his little sister physically abused by their father, neglected by their mother and on several occasions failed by the system that was created to protect them both. Alex commended Amanda on the fact that she put her daughter in loving protective hands and walked away instead of subjecting Renee to anything less than what she deserves. After seeing that it is possible to have a meaningful life with a person with special needs, Amanda made it her purpose to reestablish a relationship with her estranged daughter and Alex supported her completely. The couple knew they were going to be met with the utmost animosity about suddenly arriving and demanding time with Renee. Amanda's lawyer even explained that the only two things they had to stand on was the fact that Amanda was the biological mother and that she was invested in a program that benefited special need individuals. Alex didn't want to use his foundation as leverage to gain access to Renee, but he wanted to try anything to give the woman he loved the possibility to be with her daughter again. After a lot of deep soul searching, they both knew it was best to step back and allow Kevin to raise his daughter the best way he could but to also be an added support system for Renee. Amanda didn't want to give up on the idea that she and her daughter would eventually have that connection she so desired.

Diamond was thoroughly enjoying the time with Semaj's family, especially after hearing that they knew the only relative she never got a chance to meet. Not that she hasn't tried but the fact that her mother was hell bent on her never talking to her uncle Levi always puzzled Diamond. Shalay let her know that Levi was a complexed individual and that she sort of understood why Diamond's mother didn't want their paths to cross,

"Baby, he loved the streets, hence the reason I distanced my daughter from him, but I won't say he didn't have a heart at the same damn time."

"I'm just thankful you could tell me something about him. Anytime I asked my mama anything about him when I was younger, she would always tell me she don't want to talk about him. So, I gave up on trying", replied Diamond.

Kareem knew Levi's history just as much as Shalay, maybe more since they use to run licks together when they were younger and looking in the young woman's eyes pulled at his heart string when he suggested that anytime she's ready to meet her uncle he would arrange it. Diamond was excited but scared all the same with the idea when she thanked the Daniels for all the information because it was more than her mother would ever share. Cedric perked up the party by walking in with an array of flavored tequila shots he had made,

"Alright nah, everybody grab a shot. I wanna give a toast to my nerdy nephew for finally doing something smart and asking Erica to marry him."

"Don't do my baby like that", shouted a laughing Shalay.

Everyone downed the shots as their faces cringed from the alcohol and Alonna complained that Cedric was the only one in the house that liked tequila. Diamond started giggling as she raised her hand stating it's one of her favorite drinks to have at the club. She felt at home and comfortable around the Daniels as she began to talk about work with the ladies. They were intrigued with the stories, but the guys found themselves completely quiet because none of them wanted to sound like they knew what Diamond was talking about, except for Semaj. Shalay was all smiles like a kid with a new toy, Sherell right along with Yolanda caught themselves hanging on every word, while Alonna and Erica imagined giving their significant others a private pole dancing show. Erica started asking Diamond where she should go for a pole dancing class and Sherell was right there listened for the same info. Cedric and Khori looked at each other with the most devilish grin thinking about their women dancing for them in a skimpy outfit. Diamond explained to them that she would happily teach them for a few sessions and Yolanda was the first one to jump up, giving her new teacher her number. After seeing how interested the ladies were Diamond suggested the ladies come see the dancers in action,

"Y'all gotta come to the new spot Stagelight Casino and Gentleman's Club, a casino boat on the lake with an actual strip club inside."

"You gotta see it, place look like Mardi Gras 24/7", stated Semaj.

The gathering went on to the late hours as the family all enjoyed themselves, while Diamond and Erica felt completely at home with their new extended family.

CHAPTER 13

It's been a month since the casino and gentleman's club Diamond mentioned opened its doors, but tragedy hit the club hard. The manager, who was also a very close friend of Diamond, was fatally shot in an altercation in the parking lot of the casino. Semaj did his best to console his girl, but the loss was more like a family member than a co-worker to her. Semaj met the guy a few times and understood why his lover was so distraught over his death. Diamond's club manager treated his staff like it was his family and every one of his customers felt like a good friend, so for someone to kill him over an argument was a hard pill to swallow. Semaj had problems of his own because his grandmother's dementia escalated to the point that she had to be fed on the regular by someone. The whole family took turns feeding the matriarch for breakfast, lunch and dinner and today was Semaj's turn to spend time with his sweet grandmother. He didn't want to leave Diamond alone, but she insisted that he go take care of his responsibilities. He felt better about leaving their apartment, they recently got together, when he seen Diamond's friend Lotus come over to visit and he pleaded with her,

"Please get her out of bed. I know she's hurting but staying curled up under those covers is not helping."

"I gotchu", smiled the concerned friend.

Semaj went on his way to the nursing home, thinking of how he's going to handle being with his grandma in the state that she's in because he didn't want to look worried in front of her, even though he was. He talked to Khori a few days ago and the horror stories he had for him had Semaj apprehensive about going but the love he had for Delores gave him courage to face whatever he was in store for. It was getting close to lunch time and Semaj didn't want to just settle for feeding his senior Queen just any old lunch from the cafeteria, so he went to a soul food restaurant nearby he knew about. He got his grandmother one of her favorite dishes, fried catfish, peas and potato salad when Khori called him,

"Hey cuz, I know you probably by grandma right now, but I just wanted to check on you and Dee. Mama told me bout the shooting that happened at the casino a couple of days ago. You good?"

"On my way to grandma right now but yeah, we good. It kinda got to Diamond because she was real close to ole dude. He was real good people and that shit was uncalled for, but her friend Lotus over there with her right now so she should be good", replied Semaj.

The cousins talked a little longer, just catching up with each other, while Semaj was driving to the senior living center because Khori had to go back to Colorado for some business meetings and a promotion tour Erica set up for Khori's "Push Forward Foundation". Khori was determined to have his foundation funded by every major company in Colorado and merging with his cousin Devin's foundation "Nisha Foundation" was steamrolling the process. Semaj was proud of his cousin and brother with their generosity to give back to their community, but Semaj still held a little "ill feeling" towards what Devin said about Diamond. He still hadn't said anything to anyone about it because he didn't want to make an issue about it, but Diamond was his girl and he really cared about her. The opportunity to talk about his issues was made when Khori asked him when the last time was he talked to Devin. Semaj took a big sigh before explaining that he hadn't spoken to his brother since he left New Orleans and Khori was baffled because those two were really close. After hearing Semaj spill out everything that bothered him about the conversation he had with his brother, the caring cousin responded with a few words of wisdom,

"Dude I'm a tell you this and then I'm a let you go. I understand where he is coming from but I understand where you coming from too. That's yo girl and y'all got mad love for each other and you suppose to defend her honor all day but you gotta look at it from his point of view. He got a lil brother that makes a good living for himself, that started a business from the ground up and here comes some new female that all of a sudden wants to start her own business, after getting with you. It has nothing to do with her being a stripper, it could have been any ole female, the fact is you a giving dude just like me and Dev knows that. He just doesn't want you to get used lil cuz, that's all. But like I told you when I first met her, you got a good one in her and your brother got mad love for you dude, don't let a misunderstanding split y'all up. Learn from my experiences, don't distance yourself from family."

Semaj listened to everything his cousin said and took it all in before getting off the phone with him and promising to call Devin when he gets a chance to. He told his cousin he loves him for listening and talking with him before heading into the nursing home to spend some quality time with his grandmother.

Shalay was out running errands and shopping with her kids at the mall when she seen Amanda with her fiancé Alex. Shalay hadn't seen Renee's estranged mother since the day when she announced to the judge that she will step away from fighting for custody for her daughter. Before leaving the courtroom, Kevin and Amanda agreed on supervised visitation rights with Renee to try to start some kind of healthy relationship between the two. Shalay tried to avoid eye contact with Amanda because she still remembered the hateful things, she said about her and her kids. Fighting her was the first thing Shalay wanted to do but Khori was the words of wisdom in the matter but her oldest wasn't around to stop her this time and that anger was brewing. Avoiding to look in Amanda's direction all fell apart when she heard,

"Hey Shalay."

"Mama, that white lady talking to you."

Shalay's eyes rolled to the back of her head in disbelief after hearing her daughter Shantee acknowledging Amanda's greeting. She stood there still, with one hand clutched around the strap of her purse and the other clinched to her cell, as Amanda walked up to her. The unwanted guest asked to speak with Shalay privately, but the request was denied as Shalay's position didn't move while waiting to hear what was going to come out of Amanda's mouth this time. She was surprised when the first words to escape Amanda's lips was that she was sorry for her actions, that she was desperate to do anything to try and get her daughter back. Shalay listened as Amanda poured out about her feeble attempts to make Kevin look violent towards her or anyone that was close to Renee, so it could work in her favor. She admitted that it was a pathetic course to take and rigorously apologized for everything as she pleaded with Shalay to forgive her. Shalay couldn't do anything but laugh at the fact that this woman standing in front of her truly was absentminded to the case that all she wanted to do was cave her face in with her fist. She just reached out and shook Amanda's hand,

"No worries, we good. You did what you felt you needed to do to get your daughter back. My whole concern is just like Kevin's concerns, Renee's wellbeing is priority for us."

Amanda's eyes filled with tears to Shalay's response because the bigger woman came out instead of the raging black woman, she thought she was going to encounter. Taking the higher road to the conversation gave Shalay an advantage and Amanda took heed to her kindness because she wasn't worthy of it from her past behaviors. Alex stepped up with nothing but good things to say about Khori to Shalay and she was soaking it all in because she was so proud of the man he has become. The businessman even offered the opportunity to network with Khori on some ventures he had in mind when he gave Shalay one of his business cards,

"I don't have his number, but can you please have him call me when he gets a chance. I really would like to work with that young brother."

"I sure will", replied the honored mother.

Amanda suggested that they all go out for a late lunch but Shalay happily declined as she made her way to the exits of the mall. The more Shalay inched to the doors the more

Amanda inched with her, until Shalay just made up a lie stating she had an important prior engagement to get to. The group parted ways and Shalay headed to her car in the parking lot when her son Zachariah asked his mother why she didn't want to have lunch with Amanda. With the most unsympathetic face his mother has ever given him, Shalay responded,

"Son no matter how much the Devil smiles in your face, don't you ever sit at the table and break bread with him."

The Crescent City sky opened up to a downpour as Kareem watched the rain slam against the large windowpane of his shop. Business was slow because of the storm, except for one stylist that was braiding a young lady's hair and the other barbers in the salon were passing time talking sports. He wasn't expecting anyone to come over when Kareem heard a knock at the backdoor and after checking his security cameras, he seen it was Levi dropping off a shipment.

"Say round, you done became a UPS man now? Get da fuck outta here."

"Oh, you got jokes. Nah, I'm just helping my lady out with her new shipping and delivery service", replied Levi.

The barbershop owner knew Levi's "lady" was Leslie because he has always had her deliver a lot of stuff for him in the past, the fact that Levi was claiming her was a thrill to Kareem. It was good seeing Levi thrive at something other than hustling and made it even better when Kareem notified him that his niece wanted to meet him. Levi hadn't seen his niece since she was a newborn and was happy to set up a meet with Kareem's help. The thought of meeting with his niece was bittersweet because Levi always figured when he finally does get the chance to actually have a sit down with her, he would have his own daughter with him also. Kareem knew his friend and could tell just from his mannerism that something was bothering him,

"You good big bro?"

"Man, I just miss her. I know I wasn't always there I wasn't the perfect image of being a father, but I loved that little girl. Ronnisha would have been the same age as her right now and to hear my niece wants to see me just brings it all back. The crazy thing Reem, you telling me her name for the first time because my sister never wanted me to know her name, Diamond, that's pretty. Dude you know I did some fucked up shit back in the day, straight grimy and I'm finally trying to get my shit together but them ghost always seem to find me. I'm a make good with this one though", replied Levi.

Kareem helped his potna with the last of the boxes from the shipment he ordered, then they went in his office to chill for a minute and catch up with each other. Levi asked Kareem about his mother and how everyone is handling having the lovely Delores in a senior living facility. For the most, everybody was fine with their mother being at the nursing home, the only thing that bothered them was seeing her mental state deteriorating and that affected Levi too. At a young age Levi felt the love the Daniels children felt when he would spend nights at their house for the weekend. Any child that spent time in Delores Daniels' home received the same love and affection but also the same discipline and that was a memory that stayed with Levi. A woman not his mother or relative showing him unconditional love was a value Levi held close to him. He wanted to visit with her but didn't know if he was up for what he would encounter. Levi have seen some disappointing things in his life but seeing Delores not being herself was the one thing he just couldn't bring himself to witness. He let Kareem get back to going over his inventory in his shop and Levi told his adoptive little brother he loved him before leaving out the back-exit door into his truck.

Cedric was leaving his doctor's office after his monthly check-up with his cardiologist when Lamaj called him from school about an issue he had been having. Lamaj had been talking to his biological father Jamal for a while now because Jamal wanted to restore what was broken between them. Lamaj wasn't oblivious to all the shattered promises Jamal filled him up with when he was just a little boy, but he desperately wanted to get to know the man he shared the same blood with. Jamal had been saying that Cedric was the reason he and Lamaj's mother didn't work out. Jamal's son was skeptical of the statement, but it was a buzzing fly to his ear, wondering if it was true what his father said about his mother and Cedric's relationship being the reason for their split. After listening to his stepson stress over the idea Cedric expressed himself,

"Lamaj your mother loves you more than anyone could ever love someone. When I met her, you was the first thing to come out her mouth after she told me her name. Ya pops and mama had already split up before we ever started working together. When we became friends, she would tell me how she tried to make it work between her and him, but he was too busy doing whatever he wanted to do, he never had time for a family. You know me and you know I would never talk down on your pops, but dude is not a good person. If it's not benefitting him, he has no parts of it and son you was a responsibility he wasn't ready for at the time."

The young man listened to every word his stepfather had to say and it made a lot more sense to him than the erratic remarks his withdrawn father had laid out. Cedric was pissed that Jamal attempted such a heinous act that could have went far left field if Lamaj didn't have a good head on his shoulders. He assured Lamaj that their conversation would stay between them because he didn't want Sherell to get wind that her son had any doubt in her loyalty. The two made plans to hook up later that weekend when Lamaj comes back in town from school, just them, for some man-to-man quality time. Even before Cedric started dating Sherell, he and Lamaj would spend time together, which is a big part why they are so close now. Cedric knew what it was like to be a young black male without a father in the city of New Orleans and just being there most of the time was all most "young bulls" needed. He would always make time to just talk or shoot the shit with Lamaj, being a strong male influence and advisor when the opportunity arose. Lamaj appreciated the times and looked forward to them even more now with him being away at college. The concerned 19-year-old asked Cedric about Delores because she was the only "Bibi" he ever had and her condition was heavy on his heart. Lamaj learned the Swahili translation for grandmother in junior high and had been calling Delores "Bibi" ever since, something she loved to hear him say to her. Knowing that his mother's state was diminishing, Cedric didn't want to fill the lad's mind with thoughts of losing the only grandmother he ever known so he just told him she was fine. Lamaj could hear the somber tone in Cedric's voice and knew "she's fine" was far from how Delores actually was. Delores was everything to him when it came to Lamaj, the elder that poured love into him every time he seen her, shared joyful stories of her past and cooked like nobody's business. He wanted badly to ask Cedric to bring him over to visit but the thought of seeing his loved "Bibi" in an ailing position was something Lamaj wasn't ready for. After getting off the phone with Cedric, Lamaj went back to his studies before it was time for him to head to football practice.

Renee ran to the front door of Shalay's house from her father's car, excited to see her bestie Lenelle and rapidly knocked on the door with the biggest smile. Her face displayed the essence of joyful elations as she waited for someone to answer her knocks. Renee glanced over her shoulder to her father as if to tell him to hurry up out of his car. Kevin slowly walked up as he told his daughter to calm down,

"What I tell you baby girl? Patience."

"I know daddy, patience. I must have patience", replied the anxious Renee.

Kevin's little angel was so animated because she had her report card from school and the last time she talked with Shalay, she was told that if she brings her all A's that she would get to go to the zoo with her best friend. Shalay knew how much Renee loved animals and knew that would motivate her to do really well in school but Kevin's lover didn't know how determined Renee was to get to the zoo. Shantee opened the door to the cheerful Renee and the teen rushed right in as she hugged her, asking for Shalay so she could show off her "All A's" report card. Lenelle heard her friend's voice at the front door and made a beeline to Renee like she always does. The two hugged like they haven't seen one another in years but that was a normal event for Renee and Lenelle because they loved each other's company. Kevin adored the fact that his daughter had such a good friend in Lenelle even though there was an eight-year difference between the two. They connected with each other on a genuine level, and it wasn't someone just being nice to his daughter because she was autistic, little Lenelle truly loved the friend she had in Renee. Shalay walked in as Lenelle looked over her bestie's progress report and could hear that the challenge she gave Renee wasn't that much of a challenge for Kevin's daughter. She hugged her beau as he sarcastically laughed,

"You asked for this. You gone learn not to challenge her one of these days."

"You could have warned me, bruh. But please don't think you getting out of this, you comin' with us", replied Shalay.

In the most adorable way, Renee had the biggest smile on her face as she rambled on about how she can't wait to see all the animals at the zoo. Kevin announced to everyone that he's taking everybody out to eat, to celebrate Renee's report card. Zachariah rushed to the front door as he grasped hold of Renee's hand, telling her that they're going to their favorite spot to eat, which brought an even bigger smile. As she walked by, Lenelle let the fact that they were invited to go out to eat with Amanda earlier slip from her lips and Kevin immediately looked in Shalay's direction for answers.

CHAPTER 14

Semaj was on his way to finally meet Diamond's mother; the couple arranged a dinner at the Drew Orleans Food & Spirits restaurant and the young tattoo artist was ready to impress the way Diamond did with his family. Diamond was anxious to introduce her lover to her mother because every time she would set up a meet, her mother Darlene would make up an excuse or just cancel. Darlene was avoiding the meet because she heard that Semaj was the cousin of her brother Levi's daughter. Diamond's mother literally distanced herself from anything or anyone associated with Levi, as much as possible. It was the only thing Diamond never understood about her mother. The young couple arrived first at the restaurant and waited for Darlene to pull up in the valet section. Diamond had become accustomed to her mother not showing up when it came to meeting Semaj, but she got instantly nervous when she seen Darlene's car park in front. She latched onto Semaj's hand when her mother walked in and whispered,

"There go my mean ass mama."

"Stop it, she don't look mean at all", replied a smiling Semaj.

She reached out to shake Semaj's hand and he wrapped his arms around Darlene stating that he's a hugger. Diamond smiled as the surprise on her mother's face was priceless because Semaj was nothing like the guys her mother was used to. The hostess came to escort them to their table, in gentleman fashion Semaj offered Darlene his arm and she graciously accepted as they walked to their table. Diamond looked in amazement while her lover and her mother walked arm-in-arm, she didn't know what to say because this was not the stern stand-offish mommy dearest Darlene, she grew up around. They got to the table and Semaj continued his gentleman acts as he pulled out the chair for both women before sitting down himself. Darlene was thoroughly impressed at first sight as she looked over at her daughter with a nod of approval. Semaj poured on the charm as he asked Darlene about her career,

"So, Ms. Sweed, you're a General Manager for Housing Authority in New Orleans? How is that? Cause I know that has to be hectic, being in charge of all those complexes."

"I enjoy my job really. It gives me the opportunity to help families struggling to make ends meet and have a secure roof over their heads at night. It's not perfect but it's a start for some, especially single mothers like I was to see a light at the end of the tunnel and please don't call me Ms. Sweed. I have to hear that all day at work", replied Darlene as she smiled.

The waitress showed up with the menu for the trio and Semaj ordered a bottle of wine for everyone to enjoy as he got to know his lover's mom. Diamond pretty much sat quiet as Darlene asked Semaj about his business and how he got started. The young stud filled the conversation with aspirations of building another shop, helping Diamond start up her own dance studio and being able to just be home while making money. The exchange of communication flowed as the small group enjoyed each other's company but then Diamond mentioned that she was scheduled to meet with her uncle the next day. Darlene put her glass of wine down as she looked in Diamond's eyes with such displeasure and simply replied,

"If that's what you want than have at it, you grown and I can't stop you. As long as he doesn't come darken my doorstep, I'm good."

"Mama honestly, that's your flesh and blood. Your last living close relative. Why do you dislike him so much?", asked Diamond.

Her mother just brushed the question off as she sipped her wine and started a new conversation with Semaj, asking him about his mother and aunt. Darlene remembered growing up around the twins when she was much younger, and Semaj was stuck in the middle of an awkward situation as he went along with Darlene's banter about being amazed that two people could look just alike when she was a little girl. She told him that she would fantasize about being a twin and how much fun it would be. Semaj just went with the conversation and the disregard to the question Diamond presented to her mother but then Darlene's daughter pushed the envelope once more. As she asked her mother again what pressed her spirit so hard that she would cancel her only brother from her life, Darlene's agitation reached its boiling point. With flashes of fire in her eyes, Darlene slammed her hand on the dining table and bellowed,

"You wanna know why I don't fuck with that nigga? He killed yo daddy! The muthafucka was so damn mean that he didn't want nobody around me and when he found out I was with Desmond, he killed him. So, excuse me if I'm not all fucking excited that you wanna meet up with him cause my brother died 21 years ago."

Diamond was loss for words as her mother got up from the table and left the restaurant in tears.

Devin was chilling in his condo after practice, looking at tv when he got a call from Denise. Since their first extracurricular encounter, the two have hooked up on a few occasions and it didn't look like they were going to stop anytime soon. The young ball player would always find time to fly out to Houston to spend a day or two with Denise but they both made sure to keep their relationship completely on the hush. He enjoyed being with her and vice versa, they didn't know if it was the sheer taboo of the relationship or that they really liked being with each other. One thing Denise did know was that she wanted more of Devin and let it be known in her call,

"I'm a be in town all next week for a conference and your presence is needed sir. When I get in, I'll leave you the room number and a key at the front desk."

"You a mess. But you could just stay at my spot if you want to", replied Devin.

The two talked on the phone for a while, enjoying each another's conversation and Devin caught himself really falling for Denise more than he could have thought. She was what he was looking for in a woman and he had no problem letting her know it, but the fact of the matter was that none of his family could know about them. Denise felt the same as Devin but also knew that she couldn't share her love interest with no one, except that one time with her sister who thought it was just a one-time thing and didn't know they had become a couple. She was scared to tell Yolanda that she was still seeing Devin because Denise knew she would hear all sorts of disapproval from her big sister about the union. To be honest Denise didn't care what Yolanda thought about the affair but didn't want to hear the criticism, so she kept it to herself like Devin did. They were ending their daily call for the night because Devin had to get up early the next morning and he let "I love you" fall from his lips before hanging up the phone. Not even giving her a chance to reply, Devin ended the call and Denise stood there holding a silent phone in her hand. There she was stuck trying to understand what just happened but tickled like a schoolgirl at the remark and Denise carried that smile he gave her to bed. Over a thousand miles away in Denver, Devin sat on his couch trying to fathom what he just did. It wasn't that he didn't have feelings for Denise but to tell her outwardly that he loves her was a big step for him because he doesn't use the words lightly. To him, a person doesn't say it if they don't mean it because words carry a lot of power and to tell someone that you love them was one of the strongest of them all in Devin's eyes. He was at the point that keeping their relationship a secret was no longer an option, but he didn't know how Denise felt about it and he didn't want to jump the gun. Devin knew he was going to face some serious objection to being with Denise and maybe even some aggression from his uncle Cedric, but he didn't care. Knowing he should be in bed sleep, Devin played out scenarios in his head of what he thought would happen if he told his family members, he was seeing Denise on a romantic level. He knew his mother was going to automatically be against it because Denise is his former aunt and his aunt Shalay would probably find it hilarious that they are a couple. Devin didn't need any approval from anyone, he just wanted to be out in the open with it, but he knew he had to run it by Denise first.

Sherell was getting her little man ready for bed after his bath and Cedric was relaxing in the den looking at the news when he heard Sherell talking on the phone, but he could tell it wasn't a pleasant call. Cedric stayed to himself until he heard his wife call out Jamal's name and his attention was strictly on his wife trying to see why Lamaj's father was calling her. After the long talk he had with Lamaj about his father earlier, Cedric felt Jamal was just trying to throw a wrench in his close-knit family's mechanics now with all types of animosity. Sherell was fed up with the conversation she was having with Jamal and just hung up the phone in his face. The phone started ringing again and Cedric picked it up,

"Dude, you said what you had to say and she's done with you, don't call her again."

"Or what nigga? You ain't gone do shit! Punk ass motherfucker. You and her the reason my son not talking to me now", replied an angered Jamal.

Cedric had built up the same intolerance for Jamal's blatant attitude but instead of ending the call like his lovely wife, Sherell's husband told Jamal to stop talking and meet up with him. Scared for her man's safety, Sherell snatched the phone from Cedric, ending the call and immediately calling for Cedric to calm himself. Angered beyond recovery, Cedric stormed upstairs and Sherell thought the ordeal was over, but his stay was short lived because Cedric came back down fully dressed. Sherell rushed to the front door, blocking his exit and begging Cedric to reconsider whatever he was thinking about doing. He replied in the coldest manner for her to move out of his way but Sherell stood her ground demanding for Cedric to step away from the door. Cedric reached for the doorknob,

"You not my mama, move."

"No, I'm not. I'm much worse, I'm ya wife", replied Sherell as she stared him down refusing to move.

Cedric didn't want to push his wife out of his way, as much as he wanted to head out and find Jamal somewhere, he did as he was asked as he stepped away from the door. A sigh of relief came over Sherell as she watched her husband walk away and went out the back door to the backyard. Her heart rate calmed but her nerves was still shot as she grabbed herself a glass of wine and poured Cedric a glass of his favorite tequila, so they both could just relax. Sherell reached for the sliding door and was faced with an empty backyard, as she heard the engine to Cedric's truck start up. She realized that her husband had went out the back gate to his truck and left before she could even get to the front of the house. Sherell grabbed her phone to plead with Cedric to come back home but every call went to voicemail and tears just rolled from her eyes. She wasn't scared that Jamal would or could hurt Cedric, he was the strongest man in the world to her, but she was terrified that her husband would endanger his health by having another heart attack. After not being able to reach Cedric, she went to the best option to reason some sense in her husband and that was the level minded Kareem. By the time her brother-in-law answered the phone, Sherell was in full crying mode and Kareem could hear the pain in her voice when she begged him to call Cedric to stop him from doing anything stupid. Cedric's little brother started calling his brother's cell and the first two calls were met with the same results Sherell ran into but then Cedric answered on the third attempt. Kareem didn't want to make Cedric any madder than he already was, so he carried the calmest voice as he talked to his big bro and tried to get him to reach a state of calmness like he was. Cedric was still pissed off about Jamal but knew his car ride was just too clear is mind because he had no idea where to find his adversary. Kareem suggested that Cedric come over to his house to have a vent session with a few beers and Delores' oldest son directed his truck toward his little brother's house. He stayed on the phone with his little brother while he drove to his destination, but Cedric's tranquility quickly faded away when he seen Jamal's bright green car parked in front of the IceHouse Liquor store. Kareem could hear tires screech and then his brother's truck engine rev loud like he was speeding somewhere,

"Bro, what's going on?"

He got no response, and the phone went silent until he heard a car door slam shut. Cedric had parked his truck directly behind Jamal's car and waited outside while his rival was in the store unknowing what was waiting outside for him. A muffled sound came from Cedric's truck, of Kareem calling out his name repeatedly and the enraged Cedric stood strong in front of his truck with his eyes focused on the exit door of the store. Jamal walked out with a paper bag tucked under his left arm and his eyes fell on a truck blocking him in but then his eyes locked with Cedric's. The rage that built up in Cedric's eyes could be felt as Jamal's grip to his liquor bottle loosened from under his arm and fell to his side as he grasped the long neck of the bottle. Cedric could see the glass weapon in Jamal's hand as he shouted,

"Bitch that bottle ain't gone help you. You do better puttin' it down, cause you gone need it for later."

Jamal attempted to mutter a response, but Cedric rushed towards him, fist clinched for battle and Lamaj's father made the one mistake of relying on using the liquor bottle as a weapon. He swung at his opponent's head and like a trained boxer Cedric ducked under the attack, countering with an overhand right connecting perfectly with Jamal's chin. The night sky filled with the sound of glass breaking, Jamal's body collapsing to the ground with a thud and an old bum sitting next to the exit door shouting,

"Damn youngin'! You ain't have to do him like that!"

Cedric looked over at the old man, while he lifted Jamal's limp body up by the collar of his shirt, focused his attention back to his unconscious foe and struck him one more time with a crushing blow to the face. Cedric walked back to his truck after handing the old man a twenty-dollar bill out of his pocket and asking him,

"You ain't seen shit, right?"

"Nope. I ain't seen shit!"

Satisfied with his results Cedric headed back home ready to hear all the questions, chastising and fussing he was going to get from Sherell.

CHAPTER 15

Levi waited at the entrance of Armstrong Park for his niece to arrive when he seen Kareem talking to a young female. They were walking in his direction and the closer the young woman got to him, the more she looked like his little sister Darlene. It choked him up some because Levi hadn't seen his sister in over a decade and the resemblance was like he was looking at Darlene's twin. For the first time in a very long time, Levi was nervous, but it was a joyous nervous because he seen the smile on Diamond's face as she seen him patiently waiting for her. Kareem walked up dapping his partner as he introduced the young lady,

"Diamond, here's your uncle Ronald Levi Sweed."

"Really my nigga? You gone use my whole damn name", replied Levi as he shook Diamond's hand.

Just like Levi, she was nervous too, but Diamond's nervousness was filled with the uncertainty of the meeting she was about to have with a man she shared the same name within the uncle she never knew. Levi told Kareem he would get with him later that day as he and Diamond made their way into the park. Diamond wasted no time in asking why Levi and her mother stopped talking to each other. It was a question that was avoided until the day before when her mother dropped an anvil on the dinner table and leaving Diamond wanting more understanding of the situation. Levi knew the exact reason why Darlene removed him from her life and figured it was time to tell his side of the story to his niece. He sat at a nearby bench and patted on the seat,

"Gone relax yourself, this may take a while."

Diamond rested herself next to her uncle on the park bench and Levi ran down the strained relationship he had with his sister. He told Diamond how he was in and out of jail for various crimes at a young age and how Darlene was stuck home with addicts for parents. Levi talked about how he became very protective over his little sister when he got word that girls were being drugged and date raped on a regular basis. One of the guy's Levi use to hang with heavy was one of the main suppliers and frequent participants of Rohypnol or what other people call roofalin or roofies. Diamond listened as he painted out a picture of a very disrespectful, conniving, corrupted, rape culture mentality type of dude and then informed her that same person was her biological father. The stories Diamond's mother told her of her father was completely different from what she was hearing from Levi and the scary thing for her was that Levi's depiction of the man was a lot more believable. Diamond's uncle gave his explanation of why Darlene doesn't talk to him, but he never admitted that he murdered Desmond, Diamond's father, like Darlene claimed he did. Levi did tell his niece that he threatened her father and told him to stay away from his sister though. After Desmond's disappearance, Darlene automatically accused Levi of killing him and never talked to him again. Diamond sat there quiet as she tried to evaluate everything, she just heard but the burning question came out,

"I'm not accusing you and if you did, I wouldn't blame you. But did you kill him because he slept with your sister?"

It tore him up inside trying to find the right words to say to her without implicating himself in any wrong doings. Not that he was ashamed of anything he had done in the past but because he was trying to build something with the only niece he had. Levi's been in some intense interrogation rooms with some hard nose detectives and never broke a sweat, but he picked his words extremely careful talking to Diamond. He looked at her and smiled because his daughter Ronnisha would have been Diamond's age if she was alive. Levi never got the chance to build a relationship with his daughter and he wasn't going to risk losing this one. Diamond patiently waited for his response, hoping her mother wasn't right about him and then Levi gave his answer,

"No, I did not kill your father. Did I like the fact he was with my baby sister and got her pregnant? Fuck no, but I didn't end his life because of that. Ya mama believes what she believes because I was the last person she seen with ya pops, so when he disappeared she immediately accused me of killing him. Even had them people question me about it. Yo daddy created a lot of enemies and had even worse friends, anybody could have been his angel of death, but I wasn't that one."

Diamond left the questioning about her mother's unhinged relationship with Levi and focused on getting to know her uncle better. They walked the park, then the Treme area and enjoyed each other's company throughout the day.

        After the long journey through the Audubon Zoo with Kevin, Renee and the kids, Shalay took some time to go visit her mother at the nursing home. She was all game to go by herself, but Kevin invited himself to tag along because he wanted to see Delores too and Shalay welcomed the guest. They left the kids at home because Zachariah gets really emotional when his grandmother doesn't recognize him or his siblings. Ever since his mother told him about Delores' diagnoses, Zachariah studied up on dementia and Alzheimer so that he could better understand it but it only scared him more because he knew the inevitable outcome of the disease. Shalay tried to comfort her little man as best as she could but she was just as scared as he was with the thought of losing her mother to the illness. Kevin was driving them to the senior living center and the closer he got to the facility the more uneasy Shalay became. He reached out and held her hand, the touch seemed to bring a silence over her to the point that she felt secure. Kevin was just trying to comfort his lover in a stressful situation, but he didn't know how essential he was in Shalay's life right now. She wanted to have the strong backbone like she seen her mother brandish so many times as a child but Shalay knew she wasn't as strong as her mother was. Having Kevin at her side was her completeness and support system that held her up when she wanted to back down. Kevin parked the car and Shalay took a deep breath before he opened the door for her,

"C'mon girl, mama waiting for us."

Like always, Kevin brought a smile to her face and Shalay was ready for her visit with her mom. They made their way through the hallway and Kevin started making jokes about the elderly residents looking at him walking with Shalay. She tried to keep a straight face, but Kevin's antics were just too hilarious as he imitated voices of old people talking aloud. They were almost to Delores' room when they see a nurse along with an orderly walk out of a nearby room. The orderly was pushing a hospital bed with a big white sheet draped over it and the couple could only assume it was a departed soul under there. Shalay froze in place frightened beyond recovery until Kevin grasped hold to her hand and coasted her to the side while the center's employees passed them by. Tears tumbled down Shalay's face as thoughts of her mother being carried out of her room, but it wasn't the idea of her mother passing away. She looked around the hallway, looking for anyone that echoed a relative to the person they were wheeling down the hallway, but she seen no one in sight and that's what hurt her the most. Shalay understood the outcome to the imminent but she was afraid that her mother would move on without any of her children or family around her. Her footsteps sped up as she got closer to her mother's room anticipating seeing her mother's lovely face and Shalay heard her mother's beautiful voice behind her. The couple turned around to Delores walking towards them with a nurse latched to her arm and the smile Delores carried melted away all the stress Shalay had earlier. The nurse informed them that they were just coming back from their daily walk around the campus, which Delores enjoys doing every day and Shalay just smiled at the joy that was all over her mother's face. Delores walked up to her daughter and hugged her so tight before announcing to the nurse,

"This right here is the one I was telling you about. This is my baby Naomi."

Shalay looked confused when she heard her mother call her Naomi and she caught the nurse making a gesture to not worry about the statement. Shalay knew Naomi was her mother's deceased sister that she never met, and Delores had been talking to the nurse the whole time about her during their walk. They had all went along with Delores talking about memories of her sister Naomi, in an effort to not confuse her but Shalay had a battle going on inside, fighting back her tears. Kevin was hurting too but he managed to muster up enough strength to hold himself together in front of his love. The group sat at Delores' kitchen table, while the nurse got everyone some iced tea to drink and Shalay's mother began to ask about her grandkids. Just like a light switch, the mother Kevin remembered was back and smiling at him like she had done for so many years. The Daniels' matriarch seemed to be back to normal, recognizing everyone in front of her, laughing at Kevin's jokes and giving out nuggets of golden advice to her daughter. The time with her mother was absolutely beautiful and Shalay couldn't ask for nothing more but the extra activity to Delores's mind took its toll. She started rambling her words, not making much sense with her sentences but the final straw was when she asked Shalay her name and Delores's daughter knew it was time for her to end their visit. Kevin thanked the nurse for her service and help as Shalay hid her tears while walking out of Delores's room. Shalay wasn't saddened because of what happened but happy that she was able to spend some time with her mother, every good day was cherished.

Alonna was doing her normal weekend house cleaning when she heard her daughter Dashanae in her room, with the music loud as usual. The teen always stayed in her room, most of the time glued to her social media accounts that were logged onto her laptop and cell phone. Dashanae had created fashion accounts trying to become an "influencer" and her parents were comfortable with it, as long as she didn't have any sexual content to it. The youngster was heavy into what was in style, what was trending, and she also had her own fashion sense or style she incorporated in her fashion blogs. Dashanae had built up a strong following, male and female alike, Semaj use to tease her stating she's "Insta-famous". Alonna walked in the room to get her daughter to turn down the music but the sight she seen sent the mother into an instant rage. There was her sixteen-year-old daughter, completely naked, laid across her bed with nothing but a floral silk robe on in front of her webcam. Not knowing her mother was right behind her, she would flash a little skin every time the laptop made a money sound and Alonna lost all composure as she started swinging her house slipper at anything moving. Dashanae screamed, trying to get out of the way of the attack she was under, but Alonna wasn't letting up as she grabbed her daughter by the back of her head clinching a handful of hair. Alonna continued the onslaught of precision strikes when Steven heard the commotion going on and rushed to see what was wrong but wasn't ready for what he was about to witness. Dashanae's father seen his wife out of breath standing over a nude teen curled up in the corner of her room and he reached out to pull Alonna back but then Steven seen a turned over laptop on the floor. He looked at the screen and he could see the webcam was still on but the name across the top was what messed him up,

"What the hell is the Sexy Shanae Show? I know you not on this fucking web shit showing yo ass."

"She was showing way more than her fucking ass", replied Alonna as she threw her daughter a robe to cover up.

Steven didn't know what to say and sat on the end of his daughter's bed with nothing but disappointment in his eyes. He attempted to ask her why or what was she thinking by exposing herself to people on the internet but Alonna beat him to the question. Dashanae started to tearfully tell them that her social media page didn't start off like that, but guys kept asking her for pics in swimsuits or underwear. She said she ignored it at first but then some of the request came with money offered with it and one of her friends set up a cashapp account along with a separate fan site for the erotic request. Dashanae told her parents that she only use to do it once a week but then the more request she received the more she would perform for her paid account. The teen could see the pain she was putting her guardians through and the tears started falling more from her eyes but Alonna quickly cut the waterworks off,

"Don't start that shit, motherfucka you knew exactly what you was doing. You sixteen motherfucking years old!"

Dashanae just sat there silent because she knew her mother had had enough of her excuses of how the whole website started. Steven himself had had his fill of the situation and began to gather up his daughter's equipment. He grabbed the laptop, her cell phone, her stand-up webcam and started looking for anything else he could find that she used for her apparent webcast shows. While her husband was getting all the electronics out their daughter's room, curiosity hit Alonna and she asked her daughter how the guys was paying her. Dashanae told her mom that she has a debit card that's connected to her paid site and handed it to her from her nightstand but then Alonna noticed other things resting in the nightstand drawer. Steven rushed back in the room when he heard his wife shout asking their daughter if she was sexually active because of the pink vibrator in the nightstand. Dashanae pleaded to her parents that she has never been with a boy and that she only uses the vibrator as a prop, Steven truly couldn't take any more surprises and walked out of the room. Alonna had no more words for her daughter and followed right behind her husband as they both made their way to the sofas in the living room trying to figure out where they go after this.

CHAPTER 16

Kareem went over to check on his brother after hearing about the episode that took place the night before with Sherell's baby daddy from Yolanda. Sherell had a long talk with Kareem's woman about it because she didn't want to bother the twins with the issue because they were already trying to deal with their mother. After hearing of how Cedric found Jamal only to beat him down like a dog, Yolanda had two people she knew she had to share the news with and the first one was Kareem. Cedric's little brother knew something had happened but hadn't talked to his bro since that night. Yolanda always seen Cedric as the leveled minded one, who would keep everyone calm during a panic moment and hearing that he had a violent side for a brief minute caught her off guard completely. She tagged along with Kareem with their daughter and her niece Ashley, who was in town because Denise had her conference meeting in Colorado. Yolanda was just being nosey as usual cause she wanted to get more info on the beating of the man who is also her sister Denise's baby daddy so she could tell her. Anything that made Jamal look bad was all good with Yolanda because she truly couldn't stand him for so many reasons and this was a story she couldn't wait to tell Denise when she gets back. Kareem was just concerned about his big bro well-being and knew how easy it is for someone to be caught slipping in the city. He didn't want any retaliations to come back in the form of Jamal trying show his strength after being whipped. They pulled up to Cedric's house to him sitting outside on his porch and Kareem let Yolanda go inside while he sat outside with his big brother. Cedric knew why his little brother was there but didn't mention a thing and talked around the issue as he asked about everything going on in Kareem's life. After looking down and seeing the swollen knuckles on his brother's hands, Kareem went straight to the point asking him what's next now because they know how vindictive Jamal can be. Cedric looked in his brother's eyes as he raised up a newspaper sitting on his lap, revealing a chrome .45 and voiced,

"Negro, you forget who we grew up around? I bet not see anything out the way around me or my family. Cause if I do it's gone get holes in it first and then I'm a ask questions."

Kareem felt a little better that Cedric was attentive to the situation and attempted to lighten the conversation by talking about the upcoming football game. They were enjoying their conversation, but Kareem could see his big brother's head was on a swivel, looking at every car that passed down the street. He wanted to keep the talk they were having on anything other than Jamal, but Kareem had to ask him why he went out looking for him anyways. Cedric started to tell Kareem how the night was going when he heard Sherell arguing with Jamal on the phone and how disrespectful Jamal got with him by calling him a bitch. The fact that Jamal was talking to Cedric like he wasn't going to do anything no matter how he addressed him is what actually set Cedric off and he was fed up with it. As a man, Kareem understood where his brother was coming from and was on the same page with what he did. Kareem went back to talking sports with Cedric as they sat on the porch enjoying the nice day out. The guys were talking football when Sherell came out to tell them that she had finished dinner,

"Mike Tyson, you wanna eat? Food ready."

Kareem started laughing and his sister-in-law gave him a stare down that stopped all smiles. Cedric let him know that Sherell was still mad at him for going out that night looking for a fight, stating she was scared for his health. Kareem kind of agreed with her but also as a man knew it was something that had to be done or it would have continued, something he knew Cedric wouldn't tolerate. Cedric figured one day Sherell would understand but for now he was just gonna let her have her moment.

      Khori was seated in the lobby of the luxury Carondelet Hotel with Erica waiting on his mother to arrive. He had just finished working out the final details of a business collaboration with Alex and he wanted to share the outcome with Shalay. Shalay had her discretions about her son working with or having any business deals with Amanda's fiancé, even after she apologized for her actions personally face to face. Khori assured his mother that it was all to grow awareness to the brand along with the foundation that carried his little sister Ronnisha's name and that Alex's Vegas connections would be very beneficial. Just like every business arrangement he's been in the young man had it all under control and he wanted his mom to be on board with it because she didn't know it yet, but she was about to be involved too. Erica was looking at different florist she wanted to check out, that could decorate for their wedding when Shalay and Kevin walked up. Erica's future mother-in-law leaned over as she whispered,

"Now those are pretty."

The young couple stood up as they greeted their guest with hugs and kisses but Shalay cut all the kindly gestures short because she knew her son had important news to share with her. Khori laughed as he asked Kevin how does he deal with his mother and her shenanigans but Erica chimed in stating her lover is the same way. The group was enjoying each other's conversation but Khori noticed his mother was more concerned about why her son originally had her come meet him than go over funny attitudes. He handed his mother a large envelope labeled with her daughter's name and when she opened it the long list of graphs with percentages were all foreign to her. Khori pointed out the list of dated events with several cities on it and explained to his mother that she is now his New Orleans ambassador because he can't make all of the functions. Shalay was pleased that her son considered her as being the face for his company in New Orleans but still had her concerns with working with someone associated with Amanda. Kevin sat silent because he was just getting to the point where he was comfortable enough to allow Amanda to spend time with their daughter. He understood Shalay's hesitations to work alongside with someone that is so close to Amanda but also knew what this opportunity meant for Khori. Shalay leaned back in her chair going over in her head if she wanted to accept the challenged but expressed her concerns,

"Baby, I am truly pleased that you want me to take on the task of stepping in for you in these events, but I can't see working with someone that referred to me and my kids as monkeys. That is like the epidemy of disrespect and I just can't see myself smiling with somebody like that or someone that associates with a person like that."

"Mama, I completely understand where you comin' from and I had the same thoughts run through my head about the situation but hear me out before you dismiss it all. Levi was canceled from Ronnisha's life because of the lifestyle he chose, and you did everything in your power to keep him away from her. Because that's how you felt it should be handled and no one really questioned you about it. But did you know meeting him was Ronnisha's main goal when she turned eighteen? Did you know he was the reason I walked in that church that day and face you because I was ashamed of myself? But he made me see that family supposed to be there for one another no matter what, if they fool with you or not. Every year for her birthday he personally made sure to have a gift in the mailbox for her and she looked forward to them every year but he kept his distance because he knew her mother wouldn't allow him to be anywhere near her. Til this day he still visits her grave every year to bring her a gift and this was a man I only heard horror stories about from you when I was little. The mean man Levi, the drug dealer Levi, the no-good Levi and so forth but you as a mother was doing what you felt was right to protect your offspring. Amanda was attempting to do the same to just get some time with hers, just a mother trying everything in her power to be with her offspring. Now was it the right way? No, but can you blame her?", stated Khori.

Kevin sat back as he listened to Khori give his interpretation and for the first time he seen the other side of the story. Shalay appreciated her son's explanations and agreed completely with him but made sure to let him know

she's going to forgive Amanda for her actions, but she
won't forget them. Khori chuckled at his mother's response
but was pleased that she was more acceptable to working
with Alex's group for him. They all went to the inhouse
restaurant to enjoy a gourmet meal as Erica and Shalay
look over different vendors for the upcoming wedding.

    Devin exited the elevator and walked down the
hallway looking for the room number on the key card he
got from the front desk clerk of the hotel Denise was
staying in. The front desk clerks were so excited that
Denver's dominating defensive end was in their hotel, all
they wanted was selfies for their social media post and
autographs for their personal collection. Devin was used to
the celebrity status by now but at the moment his main
concern was getting to his woman waiting on him. They
had been keeping up with each other throughout the day,
anticipating their meet and enticing the other with erotic
words of favor. Devin's loins desired nothing but Denise's
touch and the closer he got to the numbers on the key card
clutched in his hand the greater the desire grew for him. His
wait was finally over as he quickly approached her door,
slid the key card in and walked into the room to find a sight
he wasn't ready for. All the lights were off in the room
except for the two lamps by the bedside, soft soulful music
was playing on the radio station and there was Denise
laying on the bed with nothing on but her pretty smile
patiently waiting on her beau. Devin let out a devilish grin
as he began to remove his clothing to match his woman's
energy at the present time. She watched as he rushed to
take off his clothes and she started giving him instructions,

"Slow down. No need to rush it. I wanna enjoy this view right now. Take it off slowly for me."

"Yes ma'am", replied Devin as he did what he was commanded to.

Denise caressed her skin as she watched him pull his shirt over his head, she pinched her nipples when he loosened the drawstring of his grey sweatpants and parted her legs rubbing her clit with two fingers when he dropped the sweatpants to the floor. Devin made his way to the foot of the bed and gazed at a glowing caramel delight, wanting nothing else but to devour her but Denise had other plans. She crawled to the edge of the bed where he was standing, reached out to grasp hold of the massive, hardened steak resting between Devin's legs and stroked it with her soft hands. The gentle movements of her hand only increased the hardness as she could see the veins bulge on the large shaft and all Denise wanted to do was see how much she could fit in her mouth before she gags. Devin felt her teasing the head of his dick with her tongue as she licked around his shiny helmet and sucking on it on occasion. Every time she would insert the head in, she would go a little bit further on every suck, until his tip was poking at the back of her throat and her tongue tasting every bit of him. He could feel her speed up with the motions and her excitement of pleasing him got away from her because she went one time too deep only to be slowed down by an unexpected gag. She hadn't braced herself for it but she enjoyed the feeling of the gag more than he enjoyed his dick forcing its way down her throat. Devin could feel her talents of fellatio grow to the extreme, but he also knew if she kept going that he would lose his first load very quickly. He pulled his meat from her lips like a warrior would pull his sword out for battle because it was his turn to show her his oral skills for a change. Denise was ready to finish her job, but Devin laid her back with her legs hanging of the bed, kneeled down in front of her and buried his head between her thick sandy toned thighs. His tongue found its way between her second set of lips, tasting her sweet juices, enticing him to go in for a deeper taste and his thick tongue seemed to fill her as she arched her back. She could feel him twirl his tongue around her clit, flicking the tip of his tongue against it and then going back in, sliding in and out. Devin played around with her clit like a cat would its prey until he went in for the kill and latched on her clit like it was his personal pacifier. He sucked on it, all the while twirling his tongue in a circular motion and sending Denise into an ecstasy filled spasm, clinching the sheets in her hands.

"Shit!"

She tried to push him away but the more she tried to break away, the more he pulled her to him until she just gave up and allowed him to ravage her clitoris. Devin rose after performing and before Denise could catch her breath, he slid himself deep inside her invoking a gasp as she took in every inch of him. The couple meshed together until their bodies were both covered in an erotic sweaty bliss and Denise wrapped her legs around Devin's waist as he pleasured her with his strokes. She whispered to him that she wanted him to beat it up from the back and like every other time he obeyed her commands as he turned her over. Perched on all fours, Denise prepared herself for his entrance and Devin wasted no time filling up her insides with his engorged meat. He grabbed hold to her hips, for better control and continued the pounding of her vaginal walls as he could feel every grip of her muscles on his dick.

"You muthafucka"

It was like flood gates opened up because the more he slammed into her the wetter she got until her juices were dripping on his balls. She tried to crawl away from the punishment she was receiving but Devin wasn't letting up on his performance for her to take a break. It felt like he was in her stomach and Denise was taking in every pleasurable stride he took inside of her until his strokes sped up to the point that he was about to release his creamed goods. Like from a scene to a porno movie, Denise turned around, shoved his spazzing tube steak in her mouth and let him explode down her throat. Devin wasn't ready for what she did and her final act dropped him to the bed, completely drained of any energy or will to fight her off as she sucked out every drop. After finishing off her victim, Denise giggled,

"That was exactly what I needed."

Semaj had just picked up Diamond from work and was heading over to his parents' house because Steven called him saying that he needs to talk to his little sister. Semaj didn't know what happened with Dashanae and her erotic paid account, so he really thought it was just his baby sister being spoiled again. He had no idea what he was about to walk into as he enjoyed the car ride with his lady, listening to her tell him about her day. They were planning out where they wanted to go eat after leaving his mother's house when Semaj pulled in front of the house,

"Look I'm a make this quick cause a brother hungry. I
don't even know why they want me to talk to her, that's yo
bad ass kid, not mine."

"Boy stop it. That's yo lil sister and she listens to you",
replied Diamond.

The young couple walked in the house to Steven and
Alonna sitting in the living room with all of Dashanae's
electronics in front of them on the coffee table. The house
had a morbid atmosphere to it and the gloom was about to
spread to Semaj when his mother turned his sister's laptop
around so that he could see the screen. Diamond was
standing behind her man as her mouth fell open when she
seen the bright pink screen, with a 4-way split screen,
playing small videos of Dashanae half-naked on a loop and
the words "The Sexy Shanae Show" flash across the top.
Semaj didn't catch what his mother was showing him until
he seen his little sister's face in one of the videos that kept
looping over and over on the screen in front of him. An
explosion of anger filled him as he darted towards
Dashanae's room, but Diamond halted her lover because
she knew screaming at her wasn't going to fix the problem,

"Let me talk to her baby."

Semaj waited in the living room with his parents while
Diamond walked down the hallway to Dashanae's room,
she walked into the teen's room to her sitting on the end of
her bed. Dashanae had her head buried in her hands and
when she looked up at Diamond nothing, but tears flooded
her big brown eyes as pain saturated her face. The teen did
nothing but apologize repeatedly to Diamond as if she was
begging for forgiveness from anyone that would listen, and
Diamond did the one thing that no one had done yet to

Dashanae. She sat down next to the remorseful juvenile, put her arm around her and just held her as Dashanae laid her head on Diamond's shoulder. The young lady started to spill out her heart of how her escapades started with the erotic paid site she had, how the money was rolling in for her every time she would post and how she got caught up in it. Diamond understood what she was talking about, but she also knew the obscene sexual lifestyle was no place for a sixteen-year-old girl, especially for Semaj's little sister. Dashanae listened with the utmost attentiveness as her brother's girlfriend explained to her the dangers of what she was doing along with the legal factors of an underage girl being naked on a site. Dashanae didn't think about the guys that were paying to see her undress on the webcams because she figured she would never see them ever. Diamond told her horror stories of girls who thought the same way she did and ended up hurt or worse and besides being ashamed of what she did, now Dashanae was a little scared. She never imagined that she was putting herself in any kind of danger by just getting paid to take off her clothes. Diamond asked her if she had any conversations with any of the guys outside of the site, did she give any of them any personal information or have any of them try to contact her on a personal level. Dashanae answered no to all the questions and then Semaj's lover went into clean-up mode as she told the teen it was time to erase anything that referred to the website along with getting rid of the site all together. Diamond left the room to go collect all of the equipment from the living room and Semaj immediately wanted to know what was going on, but his lover assured him that everything was going to be fine. Dashanae had no hesitation in going to the laptop and disabling the website completely, erasing any trace of her erotic show. Diamond showed her how to get it all erased without it coming back up in the future and the teen was so grateful for her help but then Diamond told her she had one more task. Diamond let the teen pick out the words to say but she informed her that she needed to apologize to her parents for her actions and that it will never happen again. Dashanae knew it was something that needed to be done but she was still afraid to face her parents and Semaj waiting for her up front. Diamond looked her in the face with the most serious stare,

"Girl if you was woman enough to bust it wide open in front of a complete stranger on a webcam, then you better put them big girl drawls on and go up there and apologize to them. Trust me, you gone need this more than them and I'm a be right there with you."

Diamond smiled, held Dashanae's hand and they walked to the living room so that they could face it together. At that moment, before any words were said, Diamond had created a sisterly bond that could never be broken in Dashanae.

CHAPTER 17

It was a beautiful bright morning, Shalay went to her angel's grave site because she had a lot to talk about with her and a lot to get off her chest. Even though four years have passed since Ronnisha's death, it is still a sting to Shalay when she wipes the leaves from her tomb stone and see her name itched into the marble stone resting over her gravesite. She attempted to hold back the tears as she started talking to her daughter as if she was sitting right next to her. Khori's words the other day stared her in the face as Shalay seen a dozen of white tiger lilies sitting in a vase next to Ronnisha's grave and she knew no one but Levi left them for her. Shalay started to express her regret for not allowing Ronnisha to build a relationship with her father and that she only did what she did because she thought she was protecting her. She started talking about Delores and telling Ronnisha how trying it is on the whole family, watching their Queen's health diminish in front of them. Shalay sat there just telling her daughter how much she misses her when she seen two women walking through the graveyard towards her. The closer the women got to her, she recognized that one of them was Diamond but didn't know who the other woman was with her. Diamond walked up to Shalay with a bouquet of flowers in her hand and introduced her mother Darlene to the grieving mother sitting next to her daughter's grave. Diamond and Darlene hashed out their issues with each other about Levi and got together to visit Diamond's cousin. They didn't even know that Shalay was going to be there and it was a nice surprise for all of them, the one thing that connected them all just wasn't there. Darlene looked down at the name that was on the stone marker,

"You seen Ronald lately?"

"Nah, I was going to ask you the same thing", replied Shalay.

As much as the two women expelled him from their lives, right now was a moment they both wanted him to be right with them. Shalay started talking about how when Ronnisha was little she would do things or have an attitude just like her father and it would drive her nuts. Darlene shared the same experiences with her daughter and the ladies laughed at the fact that Levi hadn't been around either of their children. Diamond sat back as she watched her mother reminisce over yesteryears with Shalay and was enjoying the time. Shalay said goodbye to her daughter as they all started walking back to their cars when Shalay seen her son Khori waiting at her car. It was kind of strange to see her son waiting for her but Shalay figured Khori was visiting his sister too, but the closer she got to him the more she seen the seriousness on his face,

"Baby, what's wrong?"

Khori was so focused on his mother's face that he didn't pay attention to who was with her and he told her he had to tell her something about Levi. Once Diamond heard her uncle's name, she was all ears and Khori had no choice but to share the news he had with everyone. Shalay could see the news had a lot of weight to it,

"Baby just spill it out."

"Mama I'm so sorry. I just got word that Levi was attacked last night by two men, he got away from them, but he

passed away from his injuries in his car as he drove away",
responded Khori.

How the story was told to Khori was that Levi was meeting
with two men he thought were good associates but when he
arrived in the parking lot where they wanted to meet
someone pulled out a gun. Levi attempted to get away from
them but one of the guys shot him in the leg and when he
fell to the ground the other guy began to stab Levi
repeatedly. Levi shot the guy that was stabbing him,
struggled to his car and drove off but crashed into a light
pole a few blocks away from the attack as he passed away
from his injuries. Shalay couldn't believe the words coming
from her son and looked over at Diamond with her mother
with tears falling from her eyes. Darlene was in complete
shock, her knees weakened, and she fell to the ground,
numb to everything around her. She didn't realize how
much her brother meant to her until she heard he was gone
and all of the animosity she held for him disappeared.
Diamond stood there distraught that the family member she
just got to know was gone from her life forever. Khori
didn't know what to do but hold on to his mother as she
cried on his shoulder and comforted her. Khori sat his
mother in his vehicle because he knew she was in no shape
to drive herself and asked the other ladies if they needed
him to have his driver bring them anywhere. Diamond and
her mother thanked him for the gesture, but they went off to
their car to understand the event that just took place to
themselves. Khori gave his condolences to the ladies as he
got in the SUV with his mother and he told Diamond that
they we're all going to meet up at Shalay's house later,
Diamond agreed. He sat next to his mother silent, not
knowing what to say,

"Mama, I'm so sorry."

"Baby it's ok. Ronald had a lot of demons he was fighting with. I'm just happy he's at peace now. The crazy thing is, he's finally with his daughter like he always wanted", replied Shalay as she looked out the window to her daughter's grave.

OUTRO

Eleven years have passed since Delores' diagnoses and Cedric doesn't let the time go by without keeping his mother up to date with the whole family.

"Mama it's been almost 18 years since that car accident and you was on the main line talking to the Lord about me. You always prayed for every one of us, if we was doing good or bad and it must have worked cause the kids are all doing just fine. Alonna and Steven celebrating their 10th Anniversary by going to Paris, they really turning into some global travelers ever since Dashanae graduated from college "Summa Cum Laude". Shalay and Kevin actually made it to their 5th wedding Anniversary, mama you really got you a blue-eyed blonde-haired son-in-law. I must say both of your baby girls got them a man just like daddy, will do anything for them no matter what. Mama, Kareem look like he will never quit working. Yo baby boy got three barbershops, a beauty supply store and now he got his own razors out, but your daughter-in-law Yolanda is keeping him in-line trust me. Me and Sherell are doing wonderful, as much as I work on that woman's nerve, she loves the shit outta me. Sorry for the language mama. All your grandkids are doing great. Devin retired from football and is dating Denise, yeah you heard that right, hey I'm happy for them. Semaj opened up his second tattoo shop and his wife Diamond opened up her dance studio. Khori look like he's gonna be a multi-billionaire real soon and Erica should be having your third great-grandchild real soon. Zachariah and Shantee work at Khori's New Orleans based "Nisha's Oils" CBD store. Little Lenelle not so little anymore, working on her nursing degree at Tulane University. Tre and Camille are literally like two inseparable twins, them two do everything together but they are doing real good in school I must say. Well mama, I gotta go, gotta go help Sherell with the baby shower for Lamaj's girlfriend. They having a little girl and they really wanna name her Delores. Tell Ronnisha we miss her, I love you so much old lady", was the words that escaped Cedric as he visited his mother Delores' gravesite.

Delores Michelle Daniels

1971-2048

Ralph Edgerson Jr. was the youngest of three, born and raised in New Orleans Louisiana. He always had a wild imagination but didn't start writing stories and poems until high school. Impressed with his visual writings in class an English teacher introduced him to Journalism where he honed his skills even more. After high school Ralph thought of majoring in Journalism in college but life had other plans for him. He joined the work force and writing fell to the backburner of his mind. After meeting his soulmate in September of 1995 Ralph focused on family and his first born arrived in November of 2003. 2005 came and life again had other plans for Ralph but this time on a much greater level in the form of a hurricane. Stripped from everything he knows; Ralph moved his family to Houston, Texas for a new beginning but that didn't come without trials. Thoughts of the unknown and uncertainty brought Ralph back to an old friend that allowed him to vent in a way of literary release, in 2006. It was just a way to occupy his mind for the time being, but the creation of the "Decisions" saga began without him even knowing it. In between filling out application and taking care of his family, Ralph wrote passages to a story he was putting together just for fun. His only reader being his loving wife, who enjoyed a quiet moment with the characters her husband created. Ten years had passed, and writing fell off again for Ralph as he focused more on family and work, but he still occasionally wrote poems. He met a poet on social media that really enjoyed his poems and she suggested he have them published. Not thinking nothing of it, Ralph just shrugged it off, but he did let her read over the short story "Decisions" he wrote ten years ago. She immediately wanted to have the story published and in July of 2018 Ralph M Edgerson Jr became a published author and his five-star rated urban novel "Decisions" arrived. In June of the following year, he had the second installment, "Decisions 2 True Adjustments" published, and he hasn't stopped writing since. A true New Orleans native, all of Ralph's novels are based in the city he grew up in and throughout every novel he gives detailed descriptions of the city that will always be home to him. In the beginning of 2021, he released "A Lotus Dream" and has three more urban novels being edited now. All three urban novels are set to be released in 2022. "Levi's Labyrinth" is an origin story of one of his intriguing characters from his previous novels and is set to be released in February. "Decisions Trilogy" is the finale to the saga that changed Ralph from a novice to a novelist. "Tears to Drowning Waters" is a partial biography of a friend that needed to get her story out and it was an honor for Ralph to write. Along with writing urban novels Ralph Edgerson ventured into graphic design when he created the book covers for "A Lotus Dream" and "Jahzara The Afro Girl". His "works in progress" brings him to a genre he loved as a teen, which was horror and Ralph is excited to dabble in the art with his version of scary writings. "Seeds of Laveau" will be his first attempt at the horror/paranormal genre and should be ready for release by Halloween. The next "WIP" he has in store for his readers is "Zulu Soldiers" which is still deep in its concept state, so he'll have to come back to us on a date. Ralph enjoys creating dramas that keep his readers enthralled in the storyline and hearing reader's fascination with the story and the characters. But what he loves the most is hearing the excitement from his children saying,

"My dad is an author." All his urban fiction novels can be purchased online (i.e., Amazon, Barnes and Noble, Walmart, Google Books, Kindle, etc.) He can be found on Facebook under Ralph Edge Edgerson, on Instagram as 19edge73 and he also has a Facebook Page for his books under Decisions, The Series.